THE DROVER'S CALLINGS

BY BOB HARVEY

Living Springs
Publishers

This book is a work of fiction. Any references to historical events, real people, or real places are used fictitiously. Other names, characters, places and events are products of the author's imagination, and any resemblance to actual events, places or persons, living or dead, is entirely coincidental.

Copyright 2023

Paperback ISBN: 978-1-953686-27-5
eBook ISBN: 978-1-953686-28-2

All rights reserved including the right of reproduction in whole or in part in any form without written permission from the publisher.

Dedicated to those who aren't so concerned about where they are going that they limit their options. Indeed, one can find peace by learning to be water.

LEAVING THE TRAIL

The continuing saga of the Drover's Curse ...as a reminder of the story thread. This section takes up immediately after Andy and Katie had their brief goodbye...Andy headed south on the Chisholm Trail and Katie waiting for the school board to hire her.

As she pushed the door closed, the ever-present screech of the hinges changed. It now sounded like a moan...lonely and solemn. The last whisper of the prairie wind brushed past the door jamb and the wailing ceased, leaving only the silence of the empty classroom.

Katie Munger leaned back against the door. As she did, the latch fell into its final resting place with a metallic click. Katie understood the irony...now closure had been achieved in every sense of the word.

She wondered why she didn't want to watch Andy as he rode back toward the Chisholm. She had come to accept the fact that he was going to leave sometime. Deep down inside she knew it was best that he did so...now...before he complicated her 18-year-old life even more than he already had.

She stepped away from the door. Lifting her head erect and straightening her back, she gained her composure and walked toward the desk in the front of the room with long strides and great purpose. As she pulled out the chair, she picked up the contract that was lying on the desk.......the document that would make her the teacher at Wichita's first real school.

With her reading of the first condition of employment, she froze, then trembled and began sobbing uncontrollably.

"Teachers cannot marry or engage in other unseemly conduct during their contract."

Marry? Marriage had rarely crossed her mind while she was growing up. It was something parents did, not anything that Katie was concerned about. It certainly would never be a consideration with Andy. Andy was a drover. A wanderer. A cowboy. His life was wherever he was, his destination was unknown and his schedule was one day at a time.

She suddenly realized the need to compose herself in preparation of the upcoming meeting with the newly appointed Trustees of the school. First, though, she felt the need to better understand her "unseemly conduct" during the night just passed.

From the moment that Andy had tapped upon her bodice she was drawn to him in a way she had never experienced. She quickly identified two concerns. One...he was, indeed, a wanderer. Two...he was also considerably older......perhaps as old as her own mother.

Katie had never been exposed to the emotion or tension of physical attraction.....at least consensually. There was a brief episode of having a drunken man's hands touching her most private skin. She was barely 16 and he had pulled her into the darkness of the stable and down to the floor.

She had surprised him with her strength and with the sudden and mighty impact of her right knee to his groin. The encounter was over in short order. As she left him on the floor with his knees up around his chin, she signaled her disgust by loosening some of his teeth with the pointed toe of her right shoe.

That unpleasant experience was another reason why she was intrigued with her attraction to Andy. Granted there were very few attractive and available males in the developing city of Wichita. Even if there had been an appropriate suitor, any prospect in that regard would have had to deal with Mr. Darius Munger......and even more threatening Mrs. Munger. No, Katie had been unavailable, both physically and emotionally, right up until Andy rapped upon her chest.

She already had so many wonderful memories of the man she had met only 24 hours earlier. The look on his face when he mistook her for the door made her smile. His inability to gather himself after the encounter was endearing, yes, but he was eventually able to verbalize his embarrassment and feelings in such a way that she was drawn to him.

She remembered how good Andy smelled when she stepped up next to him while he was in the sitting room. His bath and haircut were timely. He was an unusual commodity in Wichita. Clean, fragrant and not only aware of her femininity but seemingly comfortable with it.

He was neither rough nor coarse when he touched her. He had softly touched her where she wanted to be touched and when it came time to be most intimate, he was patient and caring. Her memory of the act was very complete, and she had allowed it to flood over her at least four times since the encounter.

Now, however, the treasure that was the tryst had become a burden.

She gathered herself and made an attempt to look back at the contract.

"Teachers cannot keep company with men".

MEN? Only two men mattered to Katie at this point in her life. One of them had just rode south on the Chisholm Trail and very likely would never return.

The other was her father, whom she had the utmost regard. He was one step short of being a deity in her eyes.

"Father! Oh my!" she shivered. "Father. How would he react if he was aware of my feelings for Andy. I know how he would respond if he knew of our encounter last night. Those moments must never be known to anybody other than Andy and me. Ever and forever."

A sharp knock on the door brought Katie to the moment. She took a deep breath and hoped that her flushed face had recovered enough that she could pass off the balance of her appearance as an emotional response to her hiring.

She opened the door to find four of the Trustees who were to meet with her about the teaching position. Wichita in the 1870s was still a small town, even though new arrivals were a regular occurrence. Katie recognized all four immediately and was pleased to see that they were all close acquaintances of her father. William Greiffenstein was acting as the chairman for the Trustees although his relatively recent immigration from Germany often made it difficult to understand what he was saying. James Mead had recently purchased large amounts of land and was in the process of platting the property. Buffalo Bill Mathewson had made his name as a hunter and cattleman. The lone woman, Catherine McCarty, was the owner of the town's only laundry. It somehow seemed appropriate that she was an elected Trustee as she was the only woman to serve on the board responsible for founding the city.

Mr. Greiffenstein carefully read the findings to Katie and announced the Trustees had unanimously approved her hiring, assuming, of course, she wanted the position.

Katie simply nodded yes. The men in the group interpreted her still puffy damp eyes as an emotional response to the enormity of the offer. Catherine McCarty, however, carefully studied Katie's expressions with a great deal of concern.

Mr. Mead closed the conversation with an endorsement that almost overwhelmed Katie.

"Soon many new families will be moving to Wichita, and we must be able to provide a quality education. You, as an educator, will soon be joined by others and we believe you possess the character and knowledge necessary to take our school system into the future."

With that Mr. Mead welcomed Katie into her new position. The group excused themselves and departed the building. Catherine McCarty chose to remain.

Catherine was most frequently referred to as "The Widow". She had three children, each with their own disposition.

Catherine started with a simple question to Katie. "Are you feeling well?"

"Yes, I am just flushed by all of the attention, the excitement of the new position and the enormity of the challenge."

"Katie, if you ever have a need to talk with someone in confidence, please think of me. I care for you and your family a great deal."

"I know that to be true, Mrs. McCarty, and we appreciate you and the things you do for Wichita."

"Katie, I need to ask a very personal favor. My eldest son, Henry, has been a challenge since the loss of his father. He is now too old to be attending school, but I wonder if you would allow me to enroll him? I think he would benefit from any level of education, particularly under the tutelage of a strong woman."

"How old is Henry?"

"He is thirteen."

"He is not too old to be in school. Should I expect him to be a difficult student?"

"He sometimes seems distant and uninterested, but I don't think he will cause you any trouble. If he does, you must let me know."

"I'm honored that you trust me with your child."

"I so appreciate your willingness to help Henry and we are excited about having you in charge of the school. You are a perfect match for the position and challenge."

For a moment, long enough that it was beginning to become uncomfortable, Katie felt like Mrs. McCarty was wanting to tell her something more about Henry but she nodded and said that she had to be going.

As the door closed, Katie whispered "I'll probably get an opportunity to know more about Henry McCarty in the near future."

Katie picked up the contract and read through the balance of the requirements:

"Teachers cannot be away from their domicile between the hours of 8 p.m. and 6 a.m. unless attending a school function."

"Teachers cannot loiter in town in places like ice cream stores."

"Teachers cannot dye their hair."

"Teachers cannot wear face powder, mascara, or lip paint."

"Teachers cannot wear bright colored dresses or dresses more than 2 inches above the ankle."

"Failure to abide by these rules will give reason to suspect one's worth, intention, honesty, and integrity. Faithful performances will result in an increase of 25 cents per period, providing the Board of Trustees approves."

Katie gave a small amount of consideration to each of the "cannots" and smiled very slightly as she summarized the list by saying, out loud, "why on earth would a teacher *want* to do those things?"

Katie set about her new duties with a focus consistent with her approach to life prior to Andy Graham. Her energy and organizational abilities, however, did nothing to dispel the fact that Mr. Graham was going to remain on her mind...there was a tiny space that was reserved only for him and the memories of their time together.

SCHOOL IS IN SESSION

Tables and chairs were delivered to the school building throughout the next four days. A desk arrived from Mr. Greiffenstein's store and a fine piece of furniture it was.

Katie was advised that textbooks had been ordered from Kansas City and should be arriving within the week as Mr. Greiffenstein's next shipment of goods would include the scholastic materials.

Monday, two weeks after Katie was hired, was the first day of school.

Fourteen children, ranging from 6 years of age to eleven. There was one that was thirteen..... and that was one Henry McCarty.

The students seemed eager to learn and enjoyed being in school. Even Henry seemed attentive and focused on what was happening in the classroom. He was, however, likely to sit back and avoid participation in group activities. Recesses were a challenge because of the difference in his age and size, consequently he chose to simply sit on the boardwalk and stare off into the distance.

One afternoon Katie asked him what he was thinking as he studied the horizon. Without a moment of hesitation he responded, "I wonder what it is like to go places where nobody knows who you are and then you become important because of something you do and then people respect you."

Katie knew there was a deeper message in there and she wondered what the next question should be to keep him talking.

"What kinds of important things could you do for people to respect you?"

"I could be a hero person, or maybe an outlaw, or an explorer and even a murderer."

A chill ran down her spine as she heard the matter-of-fact way he said "murderer".

"Do you think people respect outlaws and murderers?"

"Naw. But they are afeared of you then and they watch out for you and make sure they don't get in your way."

"I sure think a hero, or an explorer is a better life, don't you?"

"Probably so... but I don't know how to be one of them and I know how to do the others."

"Well, Henry, that's why you are here, so you can learn how to do those hero and explorer things."

"I'm hopin' so."

The next afternoon Katie sent home a written note with Henry's little sister.

Catherine McCarty stopped by the Munger House that evening to visit with Katie.

Katie told of her conversation with young Henry. Catherine's response was well thought out and measured.

"I have had some amount of concern about his intentions over the past couple of years. He seems to dwell on the reputations of outcasts and criminals. I even caught him trying to read through one of those trashy fiction booklets that he came upon over near the stables. He seems to think respect comes with violence."

Katie asked if Henry had been trouble for her.

"I'm pretty certain he has taken property from some other kids as I found a cache of things that he would not have been able to buy. I asked Henry's brother who they belonged to, and he was able to tell me who had them before they turned up missing."

The next question was one that Katie didn't want to ask but felt she needed to know.

"Has Henry hurt anybody or done anything so violent that it frightened you?"

"No. Never. He is very kind to his brother, sister and me. I just wish Patrick was still with us as I'm sure that Henry would be a different boy if he still had his father."

Katie asked Catherine to be very observant of anything unusual and she would do the same. "The Widow" expressed her thanks and hurried back to the laundry to catch up on her work.

THE RAILROAD

atie had heard that a meeting was going to
be held to discuss the possibility of building
a railroad between Wichita and the nearest spur of
the Atchison, Topeka and Santa Fe. The tracks were
already in place only 27 miles away at Newton.

For several years there had been talk of a spur
coming up from the Missouri, Kansas and Texas
Railway but their advancement toward Wichita
seemed to have halted at the Kansas/Oklahoma
state line early in 1871. There was also interest in
talking to the Kansas Pacific Line, but the Atchison,
Topeka and Santa Fe seemed the most dedicated to
establishing a network of rails to serve Wichita.

As much as she was interested in attending the
meeting, she couldn't because it convened at 8 P.M.
Katie knew the timing would result in a violation of
her just-signed contract. She also knew she could
count on a report... a very thorough summary...from
her father.

Mr. Munger returned home from the meeting and
reported that a group of people were going to put
money together to complete a branch line and he

felt like the group was close to having the money that was necessary. A group of local dignitaries was to approach the AT&SF officers in Atchison and the deal would almost certainly be put in place. Mr. Munger then predicted the tracks would be opened no later than the end of this year of 1872.

Katie realized that the current rate of growth was going to be nothing compared to what would happen when the trains started arriving in Wichita.

Her student body had grown to 21 students. Henry McCarty was still the oldest.

One Thursday, Henry was not in class. Katie asked his sister where he was and she said he told her that he was going to raft over to Delano, a new settlement on the west side of the Arkansas River. Delano was already well on its way to becoming the latest lawless Cowtown in Kansas Territory and Katie was immediately concerned about Henry being there.

The Widow was summoned, and a plan was put into place to send Darrell, one of Henry's sometimes friends, over to Delano and tell him that his mother needed him to come home as quickly as could get there. The phrase was sure to conjure up the possibility of an emergency and perhaps that possibility might make Henry pole his raft back across the Arkansas in a timely manner.

Darrell was taking too much time in evaluating the situation. He finally decided when The Widow leaned over and came nose-to-nose with him. "Get along. NOW!"

The crossing on raft and pole took about 10 minutes with the flow being what it was this time of year. Then the young man had to make up the ground he lost while heading downstream with the current. Once he got back to the "town" of Delano, he would have to find Henry.

Both Mrs. McCarty and Katie were encouraged when they spotted the messenger and Henry walking toward the Arkansas. They watched as the two stopped and had an animated conversation that abruptly ended when Henry threw a round-house punch at his about-to-be-ex-friend.

The boy picked himself up off the mud of the shore and headed downstream to retrieve his raft.

In a surprisingly short period of time the lad had returned, dried blood in his right nostril and a developing bruise on his chin.

"Found him in the saloon. I think he was drinkin' and thinkin' bout playing cards. He tole me to mine my own business and don't bother him again or I'll get a bigger pounding than he already got me. I ain't never talkin' to him ever again."

The Widow thanked him for trying to help and the boy left rubbing his jaw and muttering.

The next morning Henry was in school but seemed much more distracted than usual. During the morning recess, Katie asked him what he was thinking about so deeply.

"My name. Don't like my name. Don't know why I use it. Nobody would care if I call myself somethin' else. I'm thinkin' that I should call myself Billy Bonney. It sounds good when I say it. Makes me sound important."

Katie responded as best she could. "Sometimes people choose to use what is called nicknames. It's important to keep your real name for many reasons," she explained, "but you could use a nickname. You should talk to your mother about your feelings."

Henry stared at the dirt in the playground, kicked at it a bit and then responded "She don't care. She's sick. I know she is. She cries at home most nights."

"Has she told you she is ill?"

"Naw. She just doesn't seem right to me. 'Course she ain't seemed right to me since she was The Widow."

"Henry, we need to get back into class now. Thanks for talking to me."

"Can you call me Billy?"

"I can't. I'm sorry".

"Me too."

THE WIDOW AND THE KID

All night long, Katie thought about how she should ask Mrs. McCarty if she was ill.

When the students arrived at school, the McCarty's all arrived at the same time as usual, including Henry. Katie asked him if his mother was feeling better.

"Naw. She is trying to get about her work but doesn't seem good at all."

Just before recess Katie decided to make a daring move.

"Henry, I need to run an errand. I would like you to watch after the other students for recess and then make certain they return to the classroom. Will you do that for me?"

Much to her surprise, he not only stood upright but he also took a posture of vigilance...and then came the startling response.

"I would be honored to do so."

Katie hurried down the street to the cabin that was home to the McCarty's. She knocked quietly at the door. When there was no response, she rapped more aggressively.

Mrs. McCarty spoke from behind the door. "Yes, Katie? Is it something about the children? It's not a problem with Henry is it?"

"No, Mrs. McCarty. I'm concerned about you. Henry is too. He thinks you are ill."

She virtually whispered "Please come in."

By the time Katie returned to the school she knew that not only was Catherine McCarty ill but was deathly so.

Henry had diligently guided the students into the classroom and was keeping them in order.

For the balance of the day, Katie tried to balance teaching and emotions, as she knew that she would not only have to tell the McCarty children their mother was very ill but also, they would likely lose her in the near future.

She knew that the younger children would be taken care of by friends and neighbors, but Henry was a different challenge. It was unlikely that people would step up to help him because of his demeanor and personality.

After school, Katie asked the McCarty's to remain in the classroom and she sought the strength and sensitivity necessary to tell the children without causing additional pain.

After she explained the nature of the illness she paused. Each of the children was quiet and staring at the floor. Finally, Henry looked up and quietly said "I'm guessin' we already knew it, we thought it was because of what happened to Patrick....no, I mean, father".

Katie said that each of the children would be staying with friends while their mother was being treated. She told Henry that he would be staying at the Munger's for a while.

A week later, Catherine McCarty passed away under the care of a doctor in Newton, Kansas. Henry was orphaned at age 13. He never returned to Katie's classroom and was frequently gone from Wichita for longer and longer periods of time.

Just after his 16th birthday, Henry was arrested for stealing food from the store. Katie, and two members of the school board, intervened to keep him from being jailed. The Sheriff finally gave in but ten days later, Henry robbed the Chinese Laundry in a neighboring town. He was arrested but escaped two days later. Henry, now calling himself William H. (Billy) Bonney, was on the run and headed for New Mexico Territory. History would come to call him "Billy the Kid".

KATIE'S CLASSROOM

As Wichita continued to grow, so did the number of students.

The Trustees soon came to realize that 30 students meant they should hire an additional teacher. They set about looking to see if there was anyone in Wichita that could meet their requirements.

Their first mission was to determine if William Finn, a surveyor, might be available. Finn, in 1869, had created a dugout and sod shelter that allowed him to teach a small number of itinerant students. His pay during his short tenure was $1 per month. As growth in Wichita continued, Finn determined it was more economically viable to return to surveying and he, as expected, chose not to return to education.

With the pending arrival of a railroad, the Trustees decided they must expand their search and chose to look in more distant locales for talent.

Interest was to come from people throughout Kansas Territory and many of those interested had extensive backgrounds in education.

With Catherine McCarty's passing, a void existed in Wichita's leadership....a void that seemed to require a female.

Kate was frequently asked to serve on a wide variety of civic causes, and she was soon mentioned as a possible candidate for public office in the rapidly growing town which was becoming a city. She steadfastly held that her interest was in teaching and nothing more, even though others, including her father, felt that she had more to offer to the future of the region.

Late in the school year of 1875, she was visited by one of the school's trustees along with City Policeman James Earp. They advised her that one of her former students, Henry McCarty, now known as William H. Bonney had murdered a blacksmith in Arizona Territory. The news so upset her that she began to wonder if her mission had any value. For the next couple of months she would find herself wondering what might have happened to Henry had she done something different. It was a quandary that had no appropriate solutions or explanations...and it was only one of many quandaries in Katie's world...and one of the other quandaries was about to become significantly more complex.

THE RETURN

There was a very quiet tapping on the front door of the Munger House. The door opened slowly from the outside, allowing a ray of afternoon light into the living room. Mrs. Munger went to the front of the house to greet the arrival of, hopefully, an overnight guest.

She stopped short when she recognized Andy.

"Andrew, welcome back to Wichita. What brings you back here?"

"Good afternoon, Mrs. Munger. It's good to be back. Quite a lot has changed in Wichita since I have been gone."

"That is so true, Andrew. Will you be staying with us while you are here?"

"If you have room, I would be honored."

"We would love to have you."

"Is Katie home?"

Mrs. Munger offered Andy a seat in the living room, she sat down and shared the adventure that had been Katie's life since he had departed.

"A story such as that is what I would expect to hear about somebody as strong as Miss Munger," he said, choosing to change his frame of reference out of respect for her accomplishments.

"Were she here, I'm sure she would prefer you to call her Katie. School has been out for almost a half an hour. You could go by the school and say hello. Will you be joining us for dinner this evening?"

Andy's head was in turmoil, and he was having trouble gathering his thoughts so he could choose the right words.

"I appreciate the opportunity, Mrs. Munger, but I have some other commitments that I must honor."

"Do you have any idea how long you will be in Wichita?"

"No. So much depends on what happens in the next couple of hours."

"Ok, then, you go about your business, and we will see you later this evening."

"I hope so.....I mean, uh...yes, I'm sure I will" and as he turned to leave he noticed an inquisitive expression on Mrs. Mungers' face. One that he wasn't fully able to interpret.

He opened the door and, in one motion turned and stepped onto the door stoop....smacking directly into one Miss Katie Munger.

"Oh, my goodness, Andy.... it seems we continue to bump into each other at this very same spot every time you are in town," said Katie. She registered no surprise, no embarrassment, no fluster and certainly no emotion.

"Katie, I'm so ...so....embarrassed!"

"About what particular element of our relationship?"

"Well, I mean, I ...no, you...we...oh, you know!?

"I am not embarrassed. You are...and there is no "we"".

"No....I mean no....well, yes, I can see that is not true. Yes, there is no we."

"Please gather yourself and explain what you are trying to say."

"Well......What I want to say is it is so good to see you again....and that not a day goes by without my thinking of you."

Katie, with neither thought nor remorse, disregarded her teaching contract, threw her arms around Andy's neck and hugged him into near suffocation.

Katie pushed Andy into the Munger House, shoving him into a chair, pulling another one up next to him and proceeded to provide several months of personal history in the span of about 5 minutes. All Andy could do was stare into her eyes, listen to the excitement in her voice and occasionally try to put things in something resembling rational order.

Meanwhile, Mrs. Munger remained just inside the kitchen door, listening with great interest to Katie's words and being amazed at the depth, animation and intensity of her excitement and emotions.

"How could I have not been aware of her feelings for him?" she wondered.

Mrs. Munger alerted her daughter and the visitor that she was coming into the living room by delivering a very realistic, but contrived, sneeze.

"Oh, Andrew, you are back! I hope things went well with your meeting. Will you be joining us for dinner tonight?"

With no hesitation, Katie responded, "Yes, he will be here. Sitting right next to me."

"Then help me with dinner, young lady, and set a spot at the table for Andrew."

"I am so, so, pleased to do so."

SETTING THE STAGE

Darius Munger arrived home shortly after 6 pm. He was immediately intercepted by his wife and escorted outdoors and away from their home.

"My goodness, dear, what has you in such a tither?

"Darius, I have been failing in my role as a mother. Important things have been happening to Katie and I had not the slightest inkling, absolutely no awareness, let alone knowledge.

"Woman, what in the world has happened to Katie that has you in such upheaval. Is she alright?"

"She's wonderful! She has never been more alive! Darius. It's happened. She is in love."

"WHAT? With WHO?"

Mrs. Munger wasn't prepared for Darius to be as flabbergasted as he was by the news. She didn't have time to prepare for a better introduction, so she simply blurted out "Andrew Graham!"

Darius slowly tilted his head to one side and Mrs. Munger could tell from his expression that he did not remember Andy.

"Who?"

At least this time his inquiry didn't register the same animosity created by his earlier outburst, a reaction no doubt driven by the responsibilities of fatherhood.

"He was our guest a few months back. A very nice young man, well, not really young... but he seems to be a gentleman."

"What is his calling?"

One again she was caught off-guard. "Livestock, as I understand it." She felt a bit of anxiety by not being completely honest in her response.

"Where is he from?"

Somewhere her memory pulled up enough information for her to respond honestly and accurately.

"Abilene, I believe. Kansas, not Texas."

"How come we haven't heard about this before?"

"Darius, you know Katie. She is certainly not an open book. She is a private woman, and she has so many secrets in that pretty head of hers."

"Do you realize that is the first time I have ever heard you refer to Katie as a woman?"

"....and that is another thing! How could I not know? How could YOU not know?"

"Oh, no you don't. Don't you try to lure me into this maelstrom. I'm innocent and naïve."

"Such a falsehood. You should be ashamed."

"When am I going to have the opportunity to meet this stranger?"

"He is our guest and will be dining with us this evening."

"Will I have time to talk with Katie before I meet this, Andrew?"

"Most likely... but I wouldn't count on learning much about him from her right now. She is as flighty as a dust devil and I've never seen her so excited about anything in her life."

"I guess we'll just have to deal with it as it comes."

THE INQUISITION

The Mungers returned home and found Katie hither and yon. Once she saw her father she set about gathering her thoughts and preparing her dissertation.

"He's different from the young men in Wichita. He is educated. Product of an upbringing in the Army and fought in the War of the South. He's different from the other men in Wichita. He understands me in a way others don't... or can't."

Darius listened until he had no further capacity to do so.

"Young lady... and, yes, that's probably the first time I have ever used that phrase. I'm not certain what makes you so sure that Andrew is so different from the other men. I'm relatively certain that you haven't had the opportunity to get to know all these other men that you are referencing. Most of the men in this area are certain that you are smarter and stronger than they are, so they give you a wide berth. Why, then, are you so taken with Andrew?"

"He's different. He listens to me and talks to me as a person. He is a gentleman, much like you."

"Well, now we're getting somewhere. Where is Andrew?"

Mrs. Munger, who had been quietly observing the emotions exhibited by both of these people who were so important in her life, offered that Andrew would typically go over to the barber shop so as to appear at dinner as clean and well-groomed. She realized that her mention of his having done so in the past, indicated that Andrew had been a frequent guest......often enough for her to be aware of his patterns and behaviors. That was not lost on Katie and was unconsciously acknowledged by Darius.

That was, indeed, where Andrew was. He knew he was going to be not only the guest of honor but also subject to any number of inquiries about his life and aspirations. He stayed in the tub thinking and rehearsing until the water was well past cool before he stood, toweled dry and dressed for dinner.

Andrew Graham knew that he had few things to be ashamed of in his life. He was careful, however, not to get too deep in his history and he certainly wasn't inclined to start a list of shortcomings.

There was no doubt in his mind that Katie intended to assign Andrew the position as the second most important man in her life. It was important, at this time in history, that Andrew was not to be seen as a threat to the relationship between Katie and her father.

Equally important was the ability for Andrew to be able to present his background as varied, yes, but accomplished and stable.

If he could safely negotiate that terrain, then he would leave it up to Katie to explain the depths of their feelings toward each other without getting caught-up in the 'how long have we known each other' turmoil.

There was one subject that he was sure was going to come up... and he didn't yet have an answer. He had not even an inkling of what he was planning to do in the future.

Andy and Katie's feelings for each other had not been tested by time. Andy was wondering how all of this had happened in such a relatively short period of time. If he couldn't gain an understanding of the many things that had happened, how was he going to explain the depth of emotions they were feeling when it came time to have that conversation with Katie's parents?

At about that time he was thinking that hitting the trail might be the wisest thing to do but he found himself standing at the door to the Munger House. His knuckles rapped upon the door and Katie opened it immediately.

Since her position in the doorway allowed her to block her parent's view to the outdoors, she reached out, took his hand, which was still in a fist and pressed it to her bodice, reenacting their first intimate moment together.

At that very moment, all thought of Andy's riding out and escaping disappeared.

Katie took Andrew's hand and led him into the dining room.

Darius stood up from his chair and took two long strides toward Andrew with his right arm and hand extended. Andrew took a smaller step, gripped Darius' hand just enough to make a statement and thanked him for the honor of attending dinner with his family.

"It's a pleasure to see you again, Andrew, and it's always a joy to have return guests at the Munger House." Andrew read that statement as a compliment and a thank-you. Mrs. Munger translated it as Darius' reminder that Andrew was a paying guest, not a member of the family.

The rest of the family came into the dining room and Darius asked that everybody sit for dinner, pointing Andrew toward the chair to his immediate right, diagonally opposite Katie on the other end. As Andrew pulled the chair out, Katie moved around the table, asked her sister to trade places and then pulled her chair right up next to Andrew. When she slid her arm into the space between Andrew's arm and his chest, it sent the message to Darius that she had finished re-arranging the seating chart. An ever-so-slight smile appeared on Darius' face, and it was clear that Katie had won yet another challenge.

Mrs. Munger's meals were recognized far and wide as among the best fare available on the Chisholm Trail route. This one certainly lived up to the reputation.

As the meal was coming to an end, Darius suddenly turned to Andrew and signaled the beginning of the inquisition.

"So, Andrew Graham, what brings you to Wichita?"

"My horse," Andy replied with a smile.

Darius chuckled ever so briefly but immediately followed up.

"Business, I trust....and probably livestock, I suppose, since basically everything that comes through Wichita right now has the smell of steers."

Andy seized the opportunity to change the subject.

"Things are changing fast in livestock. Everybody working in my field is wondering what is going to happen when all of these railroads get up and operating. The Chisholm will be greatly impacted by the opening of your new spur. By the way, my compliments for the role you played in getting the Atchison, Topeka and Santa Fe to pay attention to you and the community's needs."

"So, you are in livestock transportation, then?"

"In one way or the other, everybody is when it comes to steers and markets."

"Well said, young man."

"I have been watching the development of the Missouri, Kansas and Texas but to me it appears they have changed their plans. A better alignment was probably the Kansas Pacific but they seem dedicated to going further south.....so the Atchison, Topeka and Santa Fe was a very good choice in my opinion."

"Well, you certainly know your railroads. I'm glad you agree with our choice."

Andrew was very happy that he spent two hours listening to O'Hara over at the barbershop. He was a wealth of information, most of it very current and it clearly would have great value in this conversation.

"So, you plan on working in that field for the future?"

"No sir. I have a bit of a decision to make."

"We all have decisions we have to make. That is what makes some people successful and the others become hired hands."

Darius stared right into Andy's eyes, looking for a message.

Andy locked eyes and replied. "Well said, Sir".

Another couple of moments of discomfort and then Darius pressed on.

"Would you please be so kind as to share the decisions you need to make?"

With that Mrs. Munger and Katie both moved to interrupt the conversation, pointing out that such a question was very intrusive.

Andrew eased the tension.

"I have been traveling virtually all my life and I'm ready to put down some roots....., the question is where do I want to root. I could stay in livestock, but I don't believe it would be possible to work out of Wichita because, frankly, I believe greater things than livestock are coming to Wichita soon. I have decided that I want to be part of Wichita's growth and that would mean a change in my employment."

The three Mungers all had very surprised expressions on their faces.... and all for different reasons.

Katie, because she had not had this conversation with Andrew and was overjoyed at his plans.

Mrs. Munger, because all of the sudden she was relieved of the burden attached to passing along slightly misleading information.

Darius, because Andrew had proclaimed that his dreams were headed in the right direction and that Wichita was indeed going to grow with new businesses and enterprises... perhaps shedding the ever-present Cowtown image.

For a very fleeting moment, Andrew was wondering if he really meant that.

"What am I saying? I have no particular skills or trade than those of a drover. Where did that come from?"

Darius complimented Andrew on his foresight and his vision, as he had indeed seen the same coming for Wichita.

Then came the question that couldn't be dodged.

"So, what are your considerations for employment?"

"Frankly, Mr. Munger I feel like I have many options. I had the good fortune of virtually growing into a young man while being in the midst of some of the greatest leadership in the US Army. As a result, I know not only battle strategies but also how to put together commodities and services... things such as foodstuff, munitions, transportation, mobilization, medical care, education, and law enforcement. I'm looking forward to reviewing the options that are developing here ...not only in Wichita but all along the Arkansas River."

The words were coming easy, and Andrew would have continued but Darius interrupted with "this community would be blessed to have someone with your background wanting to work for the long term growth of the city."

At that point, the conversations took on a whole new energy and tone. While the discussions were primarily between Andy and Darius, the strengths and input of the females in attendance were often in evidence and had significance on the outcomes of the discourse.

Toward the end of the evening, Darius asked Andrew about his experience with law enforcement.

Andrew stated that he had a good understanding in law, particularly as it applied to military institutions and their relationships with civilian settings.

"Quite frankly, I am not particularly adept in terms of handguns but very accomplished with rifles. I believe that, in most cases, a cool head should, and will, prevail."

Darius carefully weighed his next words.

"We find ourselves in a difficult position in Wichita. Marshal Meagher hired one of the Earp brothers, James, as a policeman a few years back. Then Wyatt Earp came on board when James departed. Overall, the brothers have been challenges and problems and we think we are going to have to replace Wyatt in the near future. Is that a position that you might be willing to take?"

Andy thought for a minute, staring across the room at nothing in particular.

"I have some thoughts in that regard. First, let's agree that Wichita is both now and will be in the future, moving away from a frontier Cowtown and the need for a gunslinger is going to be less important as time goes by.

"I one time had the opportunity to have a lengthy discussion with my friend Wild Bill Hickok, about what was happening in law enforcement. He said at that time, which was some time ago now, that a fast draw was becoming less and less important and I believe he was right in that assessment. I have been friends with a couple of Texas Rangers over the years and they feel the greatest asset for a law officer is the ability to communicate, maintain vigilance in advance of a developing problem and analyze every situation thoroughly."

As good as that sounded, Andy felt the need for a direct answer.

"I would be willing to consider that position but only for the short term while we find somebody that possesses both practical experience and the traits identified by the Texas Rangers."

With that, Darius felt the weight of the world had been removed from his shoulders and that Andrew Graham was a gift sent from the gods. He even quit thinking that it would be necessary to sit guard in the hallway all night long to keep daughter and guest from arranging a middle-of-the-night meeting.

WHAT WAS I THINKING?

Andy invested the last vestiges of emotional energy to reflect on the conversation with Darius. He felt his responses were well received but he wondered if he was the right candidate for the position that was currently held by Wyatt Earp.

This sleeping on an actual mattress was something that Andy was enjoying immensely. Drovers, in particular, have to be able to sleep in dreadful conditions. At best, a drover would have a bedroll that consisted of a woolen mat. The ground could be wet, rocky, snow-covered, icy, crawling with snakes, insects and all sorts of critters. Your head rest, in most cases, would be your saddle or sometimes your rolled-up chaps. What a luxury this was...a manufactured mattress with a pillow that was level, soft and warm.

Just before he faded off to sleep, Andy asked himself if he was actually invited to take the position or if there was more to come in terms of an application. His last thought was "the best weapon in my armory was my growing up at Fort Scott...and having been taught to read, write and communicate".

BREAKFAST WITH THE MUNGERS

Good or bad, morning in the Munger residence happened all at once. The senior Mungers were early risers and they clearly expected their daughters to greet the day as they did...with their missions, dress and personalities crisply available as the sun was rising over Wichita.

Andy enjoyed the morning sounds and was sorely tempted to enjoy a little more mattress-based rest but acknowledged the apprehension that he felt about his discussion with the Mungers last evening. Yes, the discourse was almost entirely between he and Darius but the entire family listened raptly. Manners, genuine interest... or both, perhaps... but Katie clearly was listening carefully, as was Mrs. Munger because she was still feeling like she missed some very important signals from Katie while this whatever-it-is relationship was developing. Darius was seriously intent because Andy might truly be a solution to a very difficult situation facing the city.

After being seated at the morning table, there was an almost uncomfortable silence. Katie was the first the break the silence with a carefully considered question that would neither lead the conversation off to the subject of the city's challenges nor anything that would lead to a sincere and intimate topic about the two of them.

Darius, having just started taking on a hearty plate of breakfast fare, set his flatware on the table-top with such emphasis that it somewhat startled everybody...including Andy.

"Andy, I invested considerable thought about our conversation after retiring last night and I feel I must ask directly if you are interested in becoming an officer in Wichita's police department."

Andy carefully folded his napkin and placed it on his lap...because that was what his upbringing taught him and because it gave him a brief period to gather his thoughts.

"Yes, Mr. Munger, I too, gave consideration to the possibility. I believe it to be a challenge...and one that I believe I am up to. I have stated my concern that I am neither an accomplished pugilist nor a marksman of exceptional speed or skill. I am, however, capable of motivating and directing people and, in most cases, that is what tomorrow's peace officers must be able to do."

"Can I consider that to be an affirmative response then," queried Darius while looking directly into Andy's eyes.

"Yes, Sir."

"Allow me a bit of time to visit with those who must be involved in the decision. I do, however, expect it to be affirmative response quickly and one that will be most appreciated."

With that being said, attention was paid to the meal and manners...with Katie smiling to the extent that it made it difficult for her to eat.

TIME TO STUDY

Andy finished his breakfast, explained that he had some appointment that needed to be tended to and asked to be excused.

As he set about getting to the livery stable his thoughts kept creating one after another consideration that required careful thought and prudent decisions. Should he be hired for the position, he would have to find a residence, as his current arrangement would create concern on the part of the city fathers... and one in particular... Mr. Darius Munger.

Next on the rapidly developing list was clothing. His very limited wardrobe didn't necessarily reflect his most recent livelihood as a drover but it wasn't appropriate for the city's newest peace officer. He decided the best resource would be found at the barber shop so he headed over to O'Hara's.

Andy found him deeply invested in pouring a cup of coffee from a crock that Daniel had just delivered from the trading post. O'Hara asked if Andy would like to share a cup and Andy gladly accepted.

"Say, this is pretty good coffee…much better than what was available at the trading post last time I tried it."

O'Hara shared that the trading post had a new owner and he was working diligently to change their image and inventory. "Seems like the new 'Wichita Mercantile' wants to be more of a dry goods store than a saloon".

"That's good news right now since I need some haberdashery that is appropriate to a new employment opportunity. I'm thinking I'm settling in Wichita."

O'Hara peered over the top of his glasses for long enough that Andy started to fidget a bit.

"So, what are you up to Andy?"

"Sorry, can't tell you just now but I'm really hoping it comes through as it would be a great change of pace, place and purpose."

"Well, our little city needs new people to settle in. I think your presence would help us to grow up. You seem to have a good head on your shoulders and your travels bring value too."

"There seems to be new construction everywhere I go. Some of the structures are very large too. I'm hoping some of them allow for additional room and board as I wouldn't be able to continue lodging at the Munger's."

"Why's that?"

"Sorry, can't tell you right now."

"I hear tell that the new building on 7th and Oklahoma Street is letting space for longer stays."

"Appreciate that information and I'll go over and see what is available. Do you know if the trading post...uh, sorry, 'Wichita Mercantile' has clothing in their new inventory?"

"I know for a fact they do as I bought some suspenders there last week...got tired of tying those straps up time and time again."

"O'Hara, you're a good source of information...and coffee. I'll return the favor someday soon."

"I'm bettin' you will, too. Good luck in your hunting, Andy."

Hoarding his pay from the fort had created quite a significant fund and when combined with the money he had salted away in the saddle bags that he recovered from the hayloft, it was probably the greatest treasury that Andy had ever built up. Now, however, it was time to see about investing in new clothing and a residence that would be considered appropriate for a police officer.

Andy made his way over the three blocks that was the route from O'Hara's to a building that had sprung up at the end of Oklahoma Street. The man standing on top of the porch cover was laying out a sign that said, "The Southern Hotel"... and a right fine building it was. Sturdy, looked like a real hotel too.

Stepping through the front door, Andy was pleasantly surprised that it was far more finished than he expected it to be.

"Can I help you, Sir?" said a voice from behind the counter that was the front desk.

"I'm wondering if you are taking residents yet...and if so, can they be longer term residents."

"Yes and yes. We weren't intending to be a boarding house, but it seems like that might be what the greatest demand is at this point in Wichita's history," explained the fellow wearing a badge that identified him as Randall, owner, and manager of the business.

Randall was concerned about the upcoming construction of the Occidental Hotel. From what he was hearing it was going to be very large and considerably fancier than the Southern was expected to be.

"I don't think we will be able to compete for the hotel business after the Occidental opens, particularly when it is planning on including a dining room," he confided, "not many dining options here in Wichita yet. Best meals in town are at Mungers but if you aren't staying there as their guest, you can't eat there."

"I am currently residing at the Munger House but I'm expecting to take a new position that will require more permanency and I would like additional privacy."

"The Mungers are wonderful people and were pressed into service as a lodging provider because nothing else was available. I expect that they, too, would like additional privacy."

Andy chuckled at the comment, particularly given the situation that he created and in which he was deeply involved.

"I will be back to you if I am awarded the new position. I will be able to afford your hotel if I get the job and I believe we will be able to get along famously. It is good for the city for you to be here as it is a very important service that you provide, Randall."

With that, Andy headed back up the street to see what the general store could offer as a solution to his greatest remaining challenge... clothing.

The building was now a business, not a pile of driftwood with makeshift furniture. It had also grown to three or four times larger than what it was months ago when Andy first rode up to it.

Daniel, the young fellow that everybody thought was remote and disinterested, was in the store when Andy walked in.

"Good morning, Andy" said the little waif that had become a friend quite by accident.

"Good morning, Daniel. How are you today?"

"I am just fine, Andy, thank you for asking."

"My goodness, what a wonderful greeting."

"I have just been hired to work here in the mercantile and I'm very happy about that."

"Good choice on management's part, Daniel. Excellent choice."

"Thank you for your compliment, Andy."

...and for the next half hour or so Andy and Daniel became even better friends as Daniel proceeded to share expansive information about clothing and the inventory in the Wichita Mercantile.

"For somebody that just started you really have command of your presentation and inventory. How did you learn so quickly?"

"I think most people see me as a different sort and think that I don't like people. Fact is I was often here in the store and I listen to what people say about the things for sale here. So, all I have to do is remember what I hear and repeat when it's the right thing to do. Another thing that I have learned is that if I am talking, I'm not listening and if I'm not listening, I'm not learning."

"You are a smart young man, Daniel, very smart indeed."

"Thank you, Andy."

Daniel explained that there was a wagon arriving in two days and it was almost entirely men's and women's clothing. Andy said that he would probably know by then if he had a new job too and, if so, he would be back.

"This hasn't been as difficult as I thought it would be. Now I need to walk the streets to see what I don't know about this town that was rapidly becoming a city...a city that may soon hold me responsible for protecting its people and its buildings."

....and that was when the gravity of the situation first came crashing down upon him, creating near panic.

OH MY GOD

"What? How? I don't have the experience to do this. How will I respond the first time I'm presented with a physical challenge or a gunfight or an argument or a robbery or a theft or......."

Then a familiar voice seemed to come from far, far away.

"Andrew Graham, I would like to introduce you to some members of the city government," said Darius Munger, while striding toward Andy with his hand extended, awaiting a handshake.

Andy tried his best to remember names and titles, but the effort was futile. By the time greetings and introductions were exchanged with one group there would be another group of two or three arriving to meet this new resident who was going to help solve the policing problems being created by one Wyatt Earp.

"Gentlemen, please forgive my appearance. I arrived late yesterday after a long ride from Lubbock. I was there to be briefed on a situation that involved a bar fight, a wounded deputy, a deceased Texas

Ranger and a mistaken identity. As a result of my meeting with the Marshal, I was able to shed light on the options available and, ultimately, we were able to solve the mysteries and resolve all of the issues related to the crimes that were committed."

Each of the men listened without interrupting and at the end of that speech in the middle of the street, each of them nodding approval. Darius asked for a vote and Andy was selected, unanimously, as Wichita's newest policeman.

NOW. WYATT EARP

Darius escorted Andy down to the Police Station to introduce him to Marshal Meagher, who had been subjected to a dissertation from Darius and who was also under great pressure to rid Wichita of the last of the two Earp brothers.

The Marshal was feeling certain that Wyatt was not going to leave without some sort of violent reaction.

The only other "policeman" in the department had cleared the area when he heard that Wyatt was going to be fired.

Wyatt was in the office, sitting behind a desk when Darius and Andy arrived.

"Officer Earp, I would like to introduce Andy Graham, our newest police officer."

Andy stepped toward the desk and extended his hand to shake Wyatt's. There was no response from Wyatt, who just sat there glaring at Andy.

"So, you takin' my position away from me?"

"Not my intention", said Darius.

"So, where did you come from, Kid?"

"A little bit of everywhere. Grew up military at Fort Scott. Dad was an officer in the Cavalry. Died in Mexico."

"I'm named after a cavalry man who died in Mexico during that Mexican – American War. He was from Fort Scott too. Wyatt Berry Stapp."

"Was in the cavalry myself for a while. Then stood with Wild Bill Hickok in Abilene and a Marshal in Lubbock. Then there was three Texas Rangers on three different cases. Didn't see anything, however, that would make me want to stay in any of those towns."

"Why to here?"

"Wichita is growing and changing. There is no doubt that it is not going to be a Cowtown much longer. It's becoming a city. Whether that's good or bad, each of us must decide."

"Good with a gun?"

"If I need to be."

Wyatt turned his gaze to the window. After a long moment of silence and a couple of very subtle nods of his head, he virtually whispered "Might be a good time for me to make a change. The folks in Dodge City want me to come over there. My brothers want me to come to Tombstone." Then, more loudly "and you're right, things are changing here."

"Got to do what's best for oneself, right?"

"Yes. I'm ready to move on."

"I'm sure the city appreciates the services you provided."

"I'm sure they do," Wyatt said, with a hint of sarcasm and a wry smile.

After Wyatt had left the building, Darius said "I am absolutely stunned that the transition was made without noise or injury. That was very well done. You are going to do just fine in your new profession. You are well worth the monthly salary of $50 that comes with the position."

Things were coming together very nicely for one Andy Graham.

SPREADING THE NEWS

As Andy walked toward the Munger's he wondered who was going to make the announcement and what kind of response he should expect.

Following a very cautious knock on the front door, he entered at the same time Mrs. Munger came into the room.

"Good afternoon, Ma'am".

"Good afternoon to you too, Andrew."

"Has Mr. Munger returned from his meeting?"

"Not just yet but I expect him any minute now."

"....and Katie?"

"She returned to the school for a time as some additional supplies have arrived and she wanted to get them organized."

"Do you think she might need some assistance?"

"I think not. She said she would be home early enough to help with dinner so she will be here any time. How was your day?"

Now what do I do?

"I participated in some very productive meetings; met several very interesting people and I feel that things are coming together very nicely."

"That is wonderful. I'm very happy for you."

Not any reference to the matter of employment. Interesting.

The front door swung open, and Darius walked in with Katie on his arm.

I was wanting to control, if at all possible, how the conversation was going to be introduced but it was not to be. Darius strode right next to me, shook my hand, and then spun to speak to Katie and her mother.

"I am pleased to introduce Officer Graham....or at least he will be after the swearing-in ceremonies tomorrow. He is not even on the payroll and has already accomplished wonderful things and made a great impression on everybody who has been introduced to him. He very efficiently, quietly, and professionally fired Wyatt Earp and everybody is amazed. What a delightful day this has been."

...and with that, everything that Andy had been worrying about faded and disappeared.

At dinner, Andy laid out his plans to relocate to the Southern and he would have addressed the issue of a new wardrobe, but Darius introduced the topic.

"It appears that you travel light, which I suppose makes sense for somebody on horseback. Do you have any idea what you intend to wear in your new position?"

"In keeping with my stance that today's lawman need not be a brawler, I believe it would be best to dress in the manner of a businessman."

"As always, that is well-thought-out....and, I believe, you have made the right decision."

With that ruling, the last complex issue was dismissed.

KATIE'S DILEMMA

After dinner Katie led Andy to the couch and asked him to sit with her.

"I'm so happy for you...for us, really...but I am in a difficult position."

"What is causing this concern?"

Katie shared the content of her teaching contract and carefully defined what would be acceptable, or not, in the public aspect of their relationship.

Andy found himself dismayed as his vision of their being together wasn't going to be possible under the new rules of which he had just learned.

"I recognized there were going to be some restrictions, both in my being a new resident and a police officer...but I didn't know that your contract puts such stringent rules on your personal life.....and, I hope, on _our_ personal lives."

"Andy, I have been thinking about leaving my position with the school system. This would be a good time to do so as we have a number of very well qualified candidates for our teaching positions."

"I'm concerned that your departure might create confusion and could be seen as a negative since it is all going to coincide with my arrival. There can be no doubt that your leaving the school system will be considered as detrimental, not only to the schools but to the future of the city."

"Whatever are we going to do?"

"Let's be patient and present our relationship in a measured manner. We will be able to learn what we, and the citizens, think about our being an 'us'."

"Father was right. As always, that is well-thought-out....and that, I believe, would be the right decision."

OFFICER GRAHAM ARRIVES IN WICHITA

The door to Marshal Meagher's office was open when Andy arrived at the Police Station. Inside, waiting, was Darius, who had determined he would like to witness the swearing-in of Wichita's new police officer.

The Marshal complimented Andy on the way he had approached the Earp termination. He then proceeded to read the content of a fairly well-worn pamphlet that was originally written for the Texas Ranger ceremony but had been edited to accomplish what was necessary for a Wichita swearing-in.

Following the ceremony and the obligatory handshakes with all in attendance, Andrew Graham, wearing the new, and very shiny, badge pinned over his heart, Officer Graham stepped back through the door and walked to the Southern, where he documented his intent to become a resident.

Next, he walked, with great purpose, over to the livery stable to round up his possessions. While there, he went to say "howdy" to his horse, who had evidently decided that there was no need to pay attention to Andy and went back to his oats without investing energy in the visit.

After returning to the Southern and picking up the key to his new home, Andy unpacked, sorted through his hiding places and rounded up enough money to fund his new residence for the remainder of the month. Next, he pocketed enough currency to purchase some new business-clothes at the Wichita Mercantile...and off he went.

THE DROVER, NO MORE

Andy walked quickly through the streets. When he arrived at the store, Daniel greeted him at the door with a great deal of excitement.

"Andy, as I understand it, the shipment of clothes from Kansas City should be here by noon. If you would like to look at some of the options that we already have, I will reserve your order when we unpack the crates."

Andy had already decided he would like to dress much like the pictures he had seen of Bat Masterson. The only things he would not consider would be boots that had too much stitching and a #5 Riding Heel.

He still had his field modified cavalry hat. Although it was virtually unidentifiable as cavalry issue it had remained with him, generally rolled up and stuffed in his saddlebags, right next to his Theodore Rains britches.

Andy mentioned to Daniel that his preference would be a bowler-style, rounded crown hat to finish off his "uniform". The two of them calculated sizes but the colors and fabric would have to wait until the shipment arrived.

Satisfied that he had done what had to be done, Andy returned to the Police Station and went about learning the ropes of law enforcement's day-to-day duties.

Shortly after 3 p.m. a little tow-headed young man stuck his head inside the station door and said "I gots a message for Andy Grim from Daniel Stallins at the General Store."

"I'm Officer Graham," said Andy, enjoying the moment, "I'm glad to learn what Daniel's last name is…".

"I's sposed to tell ya 'Yer new close is at the store.'"

Andy slipped a little jingle in the young man's hand. The transaction was new to the tyke and Andy had to encourage him to accept it. "It's to pay you for bringing the message to me. Who are you, young man?"

"Mostly people calls me 'Toad' but mah name is Tod Ketchem."

"Do you go to school?"

"Yeh, ah do," he said with his voice trailing off as he studied the coin Andy had just given him.

"Do you know Miss Munger?"

"Yeh, ah sure do."

"Do you like her?"

"She's purty. Ah'm gonna marry her when ah'm growed up."

"Yes. Me too."

Andy was startled by his statement as it was something new for him to think about. He was amazed at how easily the declaration was made.

"Anyway, thank you for message, Mr. Ketchem."

"Thank you fer the money, Mr. Grim."

... and off he went, kicking street dirt around with his bare feet, jumping over piles of meadow-muffins and studying the coin... which he soon dropped in the pocket of his worn-out, faded, handed-down-too-many-times, too-short britches.

THE CHANGE

Andy hadn't been dressed up since he was at Fort Scott as a child. From the time that he was sent away from the fort he only had "trail clothes" or military uniforms. Coarse cotton, frayed wool. Cover up or warm up.

The clothes that he was trying on at the Wichita Mercantile were a totally new experience. The material was softer and far more comfortable that anything he had worn. He was surprised that the pants and coat were as flexible as they were, not the least bit of a hindrance when moving about.

He soon had three outfits consisting of britches, coat, shirt, and vest, one overcoat, two sets of suspenders and one wool felt bowler hat featuring a jaunty red feather on the crown ribbon.

Daniel had been learning how to steam-shape hats and was becoming very knowledgeable about style, colors and value on all manners of clothing.

"Officer Graham, I have learned that many times the bowler hats are being called "Derbys" in this country. Further the higher the cotton content on the white shirts, the better it wears and launders."

"Laundry"?

That's something Andy rarely had to think about. For years the laundry he frequented most was creeks and rivers. *"Going have to change that."*

"Daniel, where do I find somebody to do laundry in Wichita?"

"There are people in town that take in clothes. I heard the other day that some China people are moving over from Kansas City and will be here soon. Now, Officer Graham, there remains three other things that you must decide on."

"Now what would they be, Daniel?"

"Stockings, Shoes, and a pocket timepiece."

"What?"

"You will find your shoes more comfortable if you have some wool or cotton stockings and they must be colored appropriately so to compliment your suits."

"Interesting."

"Yes, isn't it."

"I will need three pairs of the stockings, one for each of my outfits."

"I can do that".

"Further I would like to try on shoes of the appropriate size, perhaps two pairs to complement the suits. Not too much fancy stitching and no #5 Riding Heels."

"Yes Sir."

"Now what is this 'pocket timepiece' nonsense."

"Well-dressed men, particularly businessmen need the timepiece and a chain and a fob."

"How much are these pocket timepieces, Daniel?"

"They come in many prices and styles. I would suggest something gold plated. I can get you one with a badge design on it if you would like."

"I would like that, I believe, thank You."

As Andy walked out of the Mercantile and headed for the Southern Hotel. He noticed he felt much lighter on his feet. It wasn't because of his new stockings and shoes; it was because several pounds of coin were now safely banked in the cash drawers of the Wichita Mercantile.

HOUSEWARMING

As expected, it didn't take long for Andy to unpack and move in. Even though the room was sparsely equipped right then, it was certainly his most impressive home since leaving Fort Scott.

The new mattress kept calling to him and he soon lost the battle. He fell deeply asleep ......very peacefully enjoying the comforts of his new home, new clothes, and new profession.

Drovers were subject to a unique set of life's rules. They were mobile and unattached. While it would often seem a lonely existence, much of that loneliness was offset by a camaraderie between other drovers and, occasionally, female company that usually required a monetary investment.

By and large, there was a very limited number of "good" friends. Injury, arrest, illness, and alcohol often dictated that new teams of hands would be enlisted to keep the herds together and moving. On that rare occasion where a drover might encounter a person that they rode with before, there was very little reminiscing or sharing of experiences since they last met on the trail.

The transient nature of the career meant that drovers were often aware of things that happened, or were happening, between drives. Consequently, they often found themselves to be somewhat knowledgeable about subjects that most of the people were unaware of or disinterested in. It was this broad expanse of knowledge regarding distant locales that served Andy well when it came to conversation with those he wished to impress.

Andy learned early on that the Morse Telegraph system was continuing to expand across the country and he had been told that it was even being installed underwater and across the seas. His intent, never realized, was to keep in touch with somebody while working a herd just so he had some roots somewhere. Ultimately, he became very knowledgeable about telegraph's capabilities, and he was certain that there would be value in keeping informed of law enforcement issues in nearby towns. By working together, the various agencies would be able to monitor travel and crimes much faster than if that news was traveling on horseback.

He did initiate contact with the Marshall in Lubbock and was able to recount their conversation on the hilltop just prior to his horse choosing to return Andy to Wichita.

It was through that contact that Andy first heard about four brothers that were suspected of a number of crimes, but nobody seemed to be in a hurry to confront the Dalton Brother Gang. Andy decided to keep track of them and their travels. His dossier on the group would be of value in the future, even though there was no way to know that at the time.

THE RETURN OF A DROVER

It had been a month since Andy was installed into the police force in Wichita and, overall, it had been quiet almost to the point of absurdity. Word had gotten around that Wyatt Earp was no longer in residence and most everybody had expected that one or more of those gunslingers who didn't want to deal with such a notable gunfighter might show up to test the new man.

A few street fights, invariably between intoxicated amateur pugilists, was about as serious as it got until the door flew open one day and a young man came in breathing hard, dripping wet and shouting.

"Need help over at the saloon in Delano. Drover shot up the place, clocked the barkeep who tried to throw him out and almost shot one of the girls. He's an ugly guy and he's drunk and now he's made his way over here to Fritz Snitzler's Saloon."

Marshal Meagher slowly sat up in his desk chair, turned his head and chuckled.

"Well, first, we don't have any jurisdiction in Delano since they made themselves their own town. The fact that the drover is now at Fritz's place means that we need to go over and make sure he behaves while he's here. Officer Graham, is this something you want to take care of?"

"I can certainly check out the lay-o-the-land and see what is developing. If you start hearing gunfire, I would appreciate your dropping in to check on me."

"Most happy to do so."

The walk from the station to Fritz's is all of three blocks so it didn't take long for Andy to arrive. Out of the swinging doors staggered a man swinging his Colts from side-to-side, looking for someone, or something, to shoot, sending the people on the street into any door or alley that was available.

Andy froze when the gunman swung and pointed one of the Colts at the shiny star on his chest.

Officer Graham first shook his head, chuckled, then laughed out loud and then went into a full-guf-faw- belly-laugh-roar.

The gunman stared at the lawman, dropped his arms to his sides, his mouth fell open in disbelief as he slowly holstered his pistols.

Andy slowly walked toward the stunned scofflaw while continuing to shake his head. He stopped about two strides from the offender and then looked him straight in the eyes and said "Llewelyn, what the devil are you doing walking around shoot-ing at things. We both know you can't hit the side of a barn, even if you're standing in it. Oh, that's right, I'm sorry, I forgot... I should have said Ewing. For God's sake, what are you up to?"

The confused cowboy squinted and studied Andy's face then sat down in the dirt with a thump and started laughing too.

"Andy? 'er Clyde or whoever you might be now, where did you steal that badge?"

After they both had the opportunity to understand the gravity and absurdity of the moment, Andy walked over and helped Ewing to his feet. He grabbed his friend by the shoulders and leaned close, so he didn't have to speak very loud. He wanted to get the message across without having the crowd listen in on what was going to be a very personal conversation.

"Look, you don't know me, and I never rode with you on the trail, you understand? If we can pull this off I can keep you out of jail and get you back on the way to wherever you were going."

Ewing thought for a moment, leaned toward Andy and whispered, "that would be a good thing, I suppose".

"Hand me your Colts and walk along quietly in front of me. We're going up the street a few blocks to the police station. I'll do the talking, you just behave."

As they turned up the street, Andy saw Marshal Meagher and Darius Munger standing on the boardwalk. From their postures, it was obvious they had been more than casual observers of the confrontation. Andy touched his hat brim ever so lightly and nodded as he and Ewing continued to the station.

Once in the station, Marshal Meagher picked up a set of handcuffs and moved toward Ewing.

"I don't think they are necessary, Marshal", said Andy, when he saw Ewing starting to tense up.

"Mr. Ewing, I'm going to ask you to have a seat in this cell for a moment while I sort this out. Are you willing to do that? We won't need to lock the cell if you commit to behaving."

Ewing looked at Andy and then nodded his agreement while entering the cell and pulling the door closed.

Andy began to spin his tale. "It appears that Mr. Ewing was aware of some manipulations of the cards they were using over in Delano. When he said something about it, the dealer told him to mind his own business, or his boys would take him down to the river and teach him some manners."

"Having just enough of the Rye Whiskey that they serve, Mr. Ewing did not respond positively to the suggestion of taking a swim. He only used his Colts to make sure he had the attention of those around him and didn't intend to do any harm to anybody. Evidently Madeline, the madame and the barkeeper, said something about the scars that Mr. Ewing earned in the war down south and he was offended by her descriptions of his face and neck. It looks like Mr. Ewing then removed himself and proceeded to ford the Arkansas to get over here as his clothing is still damp and smells like the Arkansas."

Darius Munger interrupted the dissertation. "Andrew, that approach was very reckless and dangerous. That is not good police work in my opinion. He could have wounded or killed you in the blink of his bloodshot eyes."

"Not possible, sir. Mr. Ewing's Colts were not loaded. He must have emptied them out all over Delano, and then, while coming across the river to Wichita, each chamber got completely filled up with the spent cartridges and Arkansas River mud."

Andy continued, "I could tell that Mr. Ewing was not looking for further trouble. His posture and the way he moved his eyes told me he was simply looking for a way to escape a troublesome situation without hurting anybody."

Ewing's voice came from inside the cell. It was quiet, calm and pleading.

"That's what happened Marshal. I don't normally work on getting myself in situations like that. I felt bad about the things the lady said and I hate card cheaters and that was the worst whisky I ever drunk. I just got off the Chisholm up in Abilene.... that's Kansas, not Texas, and I been paid. I'll cover whatever damage there is and apologize to the lady if you will allow me to be on my way."

"What do you think, Marshal?"

"I think that was the darndest piece of police work I have seen in my 23 years. How you saw all of those things you saw and figured out all of the things you figured out is way more than I can believe. I wouldn't have believed it unless I had seen it all with my own two eyes."

On the way over to open the cell door, the Marshal finished the conversation with "I'm pleased you're here, Andrew, very pleased."

Darius moved toward the door, shaking his head. He stopped, turned his head, and said to Andrew, "This is so hard to believe. I, and many members of my family, would like to have you in our community for a long time. Just remember there is a very thin line between bravery and being foolhardy. Very thin. However, that was, indeed, well done."

Andy asked the Marshal for permission to escort Ewing over to Delano to pick up his horse and settle for damages.

On the way over to the ferry, Ewing said, "Thanks, Andy. I owe you."

"No, Ewing, we're even. I'd rather not explain. Just know that we're even."

Ewing thought about the comment and closed the conversation with "I don't know what you are doing here or where you are going with it but I just know you will be good at whatever it is."

Andy stayed on the ferry when it got to Delano. Andy returned his Colts and as Ewing walked away to settle his debts, Andy called to him.

"You do what you promised to do. I know you to be a man of your word. Travel safely. Let's not let this be the last time we stand on the same piece of ground."

DEALING WITH THE RULES

Andy and Katie had developed a closeness that allowed them to communicate effectively without using words. They used long walks in the evening to carve out time alone that created periods of interaction, but they were mindful of remaining within the boundaries defined by the school board.

Katie was watching the growth in her school and had been encouraging the school board to consider not only additional teachers but also an additional school. In the vast majority of cases, her requests were heard, and most were approved in short order.

Andy would often become a dinner time visitor at the Munger House, even though he was not a paying guest. The family enjoyed having a well-traveled guest that could share stories and newsworthy items.

Andy benefitted from the information gained from the Mungers. Their involvement in all things Wichita afforded Andy deep insight into the developing city.

During an evening porch-sitting conversation which included Andy, Katie and her parents, Katie, out of nowhere, asked if they could discuss her leaving her teaching position. She explained that she could no longer deal with the heartache that she was having as a result of hiding her emotions and feelings toward Andy.

Andy was startled by the depth of her words and spoke to confirm that he, too, was barely able to maintain his decorum when in her presence.

It was as if all of the evening noises were muted as soon as Katie spoke. The silence was only broken when Mrs. Munger whispered "I wondered when this would come up. I'm sorry we waited this long to discuss the matter. I'm so sorry for the pain you must feel."

Darius turned to look at his wife, cocked his head a bit to try and gain greater understanding to what was being said, and responded "I'm afraid I'm not very adept at understanding all of the things that go into human emotions. I have probably forgotten all of the challenges and missteps that must have occurred while we were courting. I, too, am sorry. I desperately want you to be happy. If it means having to understand you are growing up and moving through life, I'm willing. Please let us know what you need."

"I need to be able to hug the man I love. I need to be with him, alone. I want to be able to shout from the rooftops that I have found the person for my life."

A few moments of silence and then Andy replied, "I couldn't possibly have said it any better than that."

Darius asked when Katie wanted to tell the school board of her resignation.

"I want to talk to them first. I want to tell them that the rules are such that women who would be very good teachers are not going to toe the line as is required. Then I will say that if they won't change the rules, I will have to resign my position."

"I think that to be a very professional way to address the situation", Darius said, choosing his words carefully, "and I have some ideas that I need to put more time into thinking about the implications. I promise we will talk about this matter again yet this week."

With that Katie's parents excused themselves, rose from the porch and went inside for some private conversation, allowing Andy and Katie the privilege of doing the same.

THE SOLUTION

Two days later, Darius went by the schoolhouse just after school and caught Katie as she was cleaning up the schoolroom.

"Interested in continuing the conversation about your resignation?"

"Very much so, Father."

"I've been asked about the need to hire additional teachers. I tell those inquiring that the classes are bursting at the seams and the number of new citizens that are arriving, coupled with the obvious fact that many of them are with child, means we need to stop talking, quit planning and get moving....... now."

"All of that is very obvious to those of us teaching."

"I believe that the consensus is to create not one new school but two. Get ahead of the need. Wichita is not going away. It has survived the frailties of untended growth and time is of the essence."

With little hesitation, Darius continued. "I have talked with each of the school board members and pointed out that having more schools, more teachers and more students requires leadership, understanding and a strong personality. As a result of these discussions, I believe the school board is going to talk with you about becoming the Superintendent of Schools in Wichita, Kansas."

"Oh. My. I'm not sure I can do that. I don't have the experience for all that responsibility."

"Nonsense, young lady. You are already doing what you will be doing in that position....and you have been doing it very well."

"I need to talk with Andy about this."

"Please wait to see if the school board offers the position. This is a new concept for schools here and quite a departure from the usual. They might not be ready for something so revolutionary. They promised it will be just a day or two."

"Are they willing to modify the archaic rules they are currently using?"

"It appears they understand your position, but you must remember they are all older gentlemen and change doesn't come easy."

"I must think about this new concept....and I do want to talk to Andy about it. Anything that has an effect on me also has an effect on Andy."

"I thought that might be your position."

"Thank you for your faith and support."

"I pledge that for eternity."

They locked up the school building and walked home, slowly and in silence...both deep in thought.

TROUBLE ARRIVES

Andy was just about finished with his shift and was in the office talking with Marshal Meagher when the sound of gunfire echoed through the streets. Andy was out of the office, across the boardwalk and into the street first. He could see nothing out of the ordinary, so he started down to the nearest cross street.

The other policeman, Ron Smith, came hurrying around the corner, not running but certainly moving with a sense of immediacy.

"There's two guys in the street on 3rd down a couple of doors from Fritz's place. One's in the street, shot and the other is standing over him, trying to figure out what to do next."

Andy freed the leather strap that was the trigger lock on his Colt and walked toward the noise. As he turned the corner, the gunman turned to face him, gun-in-hand and red-faced.

"I'm asking you to holster your gun and then take your holster off and set it in the street."

"Not gonna' happen" grunted the gunman as he moved the drawn gun to his left hand.

"There is no sense in making this any worse. Put the gun in the holster or on the ground."

Marshal Meagher had ducked down an alleyway and was behind the gunman.... moving slowly and quietly toward the gunman who appeared to be slumping further to his right side.

"Looks like you're shot. Let's get you some help."

"Stay away from me or you will end up just like this damned poker-cheatin' thief."

Marshal Meagher called to him from behind.

"I can see you are badly wounded. We've got to get you some help or you will bleed to death."

The gunman turned away from Andy, allowing him to get a jump on the shooter. The gunman was attempting to shift the gun to his right hand when Andy arrived and punched the gun from his hand while driving his body forward and slamming the gunman's right shoulder to the ground.

The pain from the gunshot and impact with the ground was clearly evident in the groan that came from deep within the shooter. Andy had him pinned to the ground when the Marshal arrived and cuffed him. Policeman Smith checked on the man in the street and reported that there was nothing that could be done for him.

Andy helped lift the shooter to his feet and they transferred him to a cell in the office while sending Smith to get a doctor.

With a crash the door came flying open and Darius Munger, along with his daughter, came charging in.

"We heard the shot and then we were told that a lawman had been shot.....Thank the Good Lord it wasn't you," Katie cried as she crushed Andy with her hug.

Once the agony and anxiety was calmed, Katie revealed she was horrified and she didn't know if she could be married to a lawman. Darius broke in and asked "what's this about 'married to a lawman?'"

Andy took a deep breath and stood erect.

"That is something that I would like to talk to you about."

"Seems to be just a bit too much going on here right now. We should postpone the conversation to another time," offered Darius.

"Exactly what I was thinking," replied Andy.

CALL TO ARMS

First thing the next morning was a discussion on what happened in the street the day before. The Marshal reviewed the situation and said he thought everything had been done the way it should have been.

He did suggest, however, that just simply shooting the wounded man would probably have been justified and probably preferred, given the combination of factors.

Andy was uncomfortable with the suggestion as he noted that there was no indication that the gunman intended to shoot at any of the lawmen present.

"... but I know that things can change very quickly in a volatile situation."

Andy shared later that he had been thinking about alternatives to having to use his Colt 45 in situations where that much firepower was probably unnecessary.

"I have been thinking about getting a derringer for situations like that but then I remember what my friend and fellow lawman in Lubbock said about derringers... it's a lot like swatting at a hornet....only makes 'em madder.... and doesn't stop them."

"A couple years back I was in the Territorial Capitol over around Lawrence and there was a dust-up between a couple of hired gunmen and one of the anti-slavery people, a black fellow named Sam Woods. He used a club of some sort to waylay those guys...and in short order, too. It was shaped like something a person could use to lean on while walking. I told O'Hara about the club, and he said many people in Europe use them for protection.... called it a fancier name that didn't mean anything to me. It was quick and final in my way of thinking. Found out later that he always carried the thing, he didn't carry firearms and was widely known as a force to be reckoned with. I'm thinking about looking into that concept. What do you think Marshal?"

"I'm alright with anything that doesn't get you shot."

"I need to give some thought to this."

NOW, TO THE MATTER(S) AT HAND

For the next day, Andy steered clear of Darius Munger. He wasn't sure why, exactly, but he didn't think he was ready to ask for Katie's hand.

Darius, for his part, didn't know how he would respond. He so wanted Katie to be happy, he very much approved of Andy, even in his law enforcement position, he knew his wife would bless the union but, after all, Katie was his oldest.

Katie had just unlocked the door at the school when three of the school board members arrived. Katie, not one to be flustered, was taken back by the stealth of their visit.

"I suppose you are here to talk about my opinions on the rules of the teaching contract?"

President of the Board was still William Greiffenstein and it was still difficult to understand his thick German accent.

"Yes, Mr. Munger has shared your opinion and concern. Frankly it caught us off guard and we are not sure how to proceed." Sensing that Katie was having trouble understanding, his voice tailed off to nothing.

Board Member James Mead then took over the role of moderator.

"To our knowledge these rules are used by most schools, and they are consistent with the those of the finest of schools."

"I believe that to be true, but I think it is time to change the rules to accommodate the necessary changes in today's women. We need to attract women to teach our rapidly growing population." Katie knew that sounded a bit like pleading and she started to apologize.

"We are concerned that it comes across as some sort of ultimatum."

"It should...because it is."

"So, you would resign from your position if we don't acquiesce and change the rules?"

"Yes, I would."

"I'm afraid that we have been remiss in our attempts to replace the late Catherine McCarty on our school board. Frankly we haven't been able to find an appropriate candidate for that spot."

"Are you saying that you can't find an appropriate candidate... or should I specifically cite that it must be a 'woman' for the vacancy?"

"Yes, I suppose we should specify that we are seeking a woman."

"If we could change these archaic rules to allow a woman to grow as she should, there would be numerous candidates with the drive, spirit and experience for these positions."

"Yes, perhaps."

"What are you going to do?"

"At the very least, we would like you to accept the vacant position on the Board if you chose to resign... but we would like you to consider becoming the new Superintendent of Schools for Wichita. We feel we need your strengths to take our schools forward.

"I have given considerable thought to that position. I would be honored to serve as your Superintendent. I will ask that you allow me to provide an appropriate candidate for the Board position, however, as it is inappropriate to serve in both positions."

Greiffenstein took a deep breath, stood erect and said, "Are we in agreement then?"

"Yes, I will start creating a contract for the Superintendents position immediately. Thank you for your kindness and support."

With their departure came the realization that another challenge had presented itself but, regardless of its importance, it was not of the same gravity as the discussion she knew she had to have with her parents and the love of her life.

Katie somehow maintained her composure throughout the school day and found herself becoming increasingly concerned about what was to come.

ONE STEP AT A TIME

Katie arrived home just a bit later than usual and was surprised to find that no one was at home. Her mother was very protective of daily rituals as she looked forward to cooking the evening meal but, this day, was nowhere to be found.

Katie decided that perhaps she would walk over to her father's office to see if, perhaps, her mother was talking with him about the meeting that was to take place.

As she stepped into the street, she spotted Policeman Andrew Graham, mounted on his horse, coming around the corner.

"Good afternoon, Policeman Graham. It is very nice to see you patrolling the streets, keeping everybody safe."

"Good afternoon, Superintendent Munger, may I be among the first to offer my congratulations on your new position."

Surprised that the information was already out of the streets, she was somewhat taken aback.

"How does that happen in this sleepy little Cowtown?"

"You have a following, I believe."

"Have you seen my mother or father?"

"Yes, they are visiting the Perkins cabin out west on the Little Arkansas."

"Why?"

"Something about buying it so we will have a home in which to live after we're married."

"WHAT?"

"I talked with your father earlier today. The discussion was short but cordial."

"...and he accepted your.........?"

"Our."

"OUR betrothal?"

"Now if you will accept my proposal, we can start making plans."

"Oh Andy! Of course, I do."

"Good, now swing up here and let's go out to the cabin for an inspection."

"I can't."

"Why?"

"I'm wearing a skirt".

"Time to start breaking some rules."

"OK, give me your hand."

"I am honored to do so...in every sense of the phrase."

THE FUTURE HOME

The Perkins family had settled the homestead several years earlier. Caleb Perkins was very handy with an axe and almost every wood-working tool ever invented...they also had four children, so he built a cabin which was larger than the norm.

The home was two-thirds family living and the remainder consisted of three bedrooms that provided adequate space and privacy.

There was little need for discussion or negotiation and soon the party of four was enroute back to Wichita.... a distance of little more than a mile but it also required a crossing of the Little Arkansas. This time of year, it was easily forded at "the shallows" but to be a full-time home, the property would have to be improved to provide a bridge or, at least, a ferry.

Once on the eastern bank, Darius studied the area. "It will take a bit of doing but it appears to me that a wooden bridge flanked by stones could be built there between those two hills," he said, gesturing to the south and east.

"The railroad surveyors are a couple miles outside of town doing their work for the rail route. I'll ask them to look at the possibilities and give us some direction," he nodded, with a smile expressing his satisfaction with the plan.

Katie was sitting side-saddle on the rump of Andy's horse. As they neared the Munger house, Katie told Andy that she was glad the horse had been ridden little recently. It had become softer and wider than a drover's horse would be, and for that she was thankful.

"I'm sure," Andy replied, with a wry smile, all the time knowing he would have to make a schedule to work with the horse, who had already become less than excited about being ridden on those rare occasions when Andy took him from the stable.

Andy didn't know just how prophetic his thoughts were. "You just never know when I might have to take to the trails once again."

BACK ON THE TRAIL

Andy had developed a ritual that involved walking the two main streets each morning on the way to the office. It allowed him to survey the changes that were taking place all over Wichita on a daily basis and he had developed a number of close friends in the growing city. Once he finished his daily patrol, he returned to the police station and reported to whomever was in the office when he arrived. Most times it was only Marshal Meagher but sometimes Officer Smith was also in.

This day, only Marshal Meagher was in and sitting at his desk, studying a single piece of paper that looked to be a telegram.

"Just got this from down in Oklahoma Territory. Can't say that I know this fellow for certain but for some reason the name is familiar. I think he is a Texas Ranger, though he doesn't say so," the Marshal said with an air of quiet reflection.

"...Says he will be here today or tomorrow and would like to meet with me and my deputies. Not sure what that means."

Andy studied him for a while then responded. "It has been quite some time since I laid eyes on a Texas Ranger. I hear tell they have been going through lots of changes now that the country is becoming more settled. Most towns of any size have their own lawmen. The Rangers don't have to uphold the law in most all of the country anymore."

"True, that is," said the Marshal.

Andy took his leave and walked toward the area where the new school would be built. From the freshly dug reference holes, it was going to be quite a structure.

While leaning up against one of the many trees that had been planted to restore some shade in Wichita, he spotted a lone rider easing along 3rd. From his vantage point he was able to get a good look at the rider without being very visible to the newcomer.

Andy was thinking there was something familiar about the rider... *"the horse and the rider are a good pair, no badge or evidence there ever was one, two straight holsters with 45's, side knife and a Henry rifle in the scabbard. The rider was alert but not outwardly surveying the public or the buildings. Surely could be a drover just riding through...but I think I'll head back and look through the wanted posters."*

Andy returned to the office and shared the sighting with Meagher.

"So, what you're saying is there is something familiar about the man but no reason to be wary. I encourage you, however, to review the posters.... if nothing else but to grow more familiar with the men who ARE in the stack," he said, in a somewhat offhand manner.

The front door hardware rattled then went quiet. Then the door slowly opened. In what seemed to be an extraordinarily long time, the visitor stepped into the room. It was the rider Andy had noticed and he went on alert.

"Good day, gentlemen."

"How can we help you?" asked the Marshal.

"My name is Inspector Richard Brockman and I have come to ask your assistance."

Everything clicked into place once the rider started talking. It was the same Texas Ranger that had dispatched August Carelton, his brother and his weasel-like henchman several months ago in the Arickaree Breaks up near Nebraska.

Andy stepped forward and extended his hand.

"It is a pleasure to meet up with you again, Inspector Brockman. Last time we met you were a Texas Ranger and you captured, in a very permanent manner, two of three fellows that were intent on killing me. Further you provided me with a horse and pulled cactus needles out of my ear," explained Andy.

Brockman studied Andy for an extended period of time then a slow smile came to his face.

"Ah, yes. As I remember it, there was quite a large area of land covered with bodies....considerably more than I would have expected, especially since you didn't have anything but a Colt 45 packed full of dirt and a rattlesnake demanding your attention," Brockman offered, with a much greater smile now.

"Yes, that was the event."

"Well, judging by the badge and your location, many things have changed for you, just as they have for me."

The Marshal interrupted the reunion.

"I guess I can safely assume that you are no longer a Ranger," he said, carefully choosing his words.

"You are correct, Marshal."

"What can we help you with, then."

"I am under contract to a cattlemen's organization in Oklahoma Territory and I have been asked to figure out who is rustling cattle and killing drovers in the process."

Andy sat bolt upright with the mention of drovers being killed as he knew many of the men working the herds.

"How can we help you with this investigation?"

"I need a drover who can go on the trail...not with the herds, but with these rustlers. I need someone who can find out who is ramrodding this gang so we can round up him and his men. We know that most of the thieving drovers are from Amarillo and Lubbock. Most of the drives are going up that way now because there isn't much grass left over here on the Chisholm. The rustling and shootings are happening near Colorado Territory and stock is moving both north and south from there."

"I come from a drover background in the way-back. Been years now but I still remember how to do it or at least talk about it," Andy interjected, being careful not to bring too much background information to the fore.

"What do you think Marshal?" Andy asked, thinking about friends that might have been killed or injured.

"I can't send you as an officer from Wichita. You would have to leave the department."

Andy asked Brockman if he would be riding along on the search.

"Can't be anywhere close," he replied, "Too many of these people know who I am due to my having been a Ranger. I would be found out...and likely dead...in no time."

Andy suddenly found himself challenged by his developing life.

His mind clicked off the reasons not to go. *"It wouldn't make any sense to do this. I have so many things going my way. No reason, at all, to do this."*

"I need to talk this over with others. When do you need a decision?"

"The longer we delay, the more men they recruit, and the more people lose their lives."

"Let's meet tomorrow and I'll give you my answer. How long will it take to get the information we need?"

"Hmmm. Let's figure 9 or 10 days ride to Amarillo. Couple of days hanging around the streets and saloons. Couple of days getting in on a rustling raid.

Day or two to lose your job and then ride like hell to save your life. Could be about three weeks, I'm thinkin'."

"Ok. Let's talk tomorrow."

"Fine with me. Tomorrow it is then. By your leave, Marshal."

"Good day, Inspector."

...and then he was out the door. The Marshal sat in his chair, studying Andy and shaking his head.

"'Bout the first time I ever doubted your sanity and judgement."

"Would you be willing to hold my job until I'm back?"

"Can't say that I will. Mostly because I don't know if you will make it back."

"I have to talk with the Mungers."

"I can't say I think that is a good idea."

"I don't know that I have a choice in the matter."

"Of course, you do. No need to go out searching for danger."

"I have so many friends that are drovers, I'm concerned about their safety."

"...and your dying is going to make a difference?"

"Maybe...but I have no intention of dying. My military training should be of value."

"Maybe...but I'm not hearing anything about an army or a posse or anything. You will be all by yourself."

"I have to talk to the Mungers."

"Be a mistake, it will."

"May well be," he said as he headed out the door.

Andy decided his first stop would be at the schoolhouse to have a private conversation with Katie. He wasn't in her presence for more than a few seconds before she sensed the coming storm.

"I have been asked to assist a lawman from Oklahoma in investigating over around Amarillo. It will likely be a couple of weeks and I wouldn't consider it except for he saved my life once and I expect I know a number of drovers who are being killed while a group of outlaws are rustling livestock," Andy reported, knowing that the actual story would be more than Katie should know.

"Andy, that sounds very dangerous."

"I know of the need to be careful and diligent."

"Why would you even consider this given the things we have coming into our lives?".

"Concern about others and commitment to my profession."

"What about your concern to me and your commitment to our lives together?".

"It will be a brief undertaking and then we will return to building of our lives."

"Andy, please don't do this."

"I need to talk with your father."

"No, Andy, don't do that. He won't understand."

"I'll give this more thought. I have to give them an answer in the morning."

"You can give them any answer you want to at any time you like. I do not want you putting yourself in harm's way...and I certainly will not encourage this foolhardy expedition."

....and with that comment, one that kept echoing in his ears, Andy excused himself from Katie's presence and stormed out of the school, intent on returning to his room at the Southern Hotel, where he spent the night tossing and turning and wondering why he was even considering such nonsense.

With the rising of the sun, Andy dug into his saddlebags and recovered his clothing from his days as a drover. He slipped them on, went downstairs to pay for his room for the next 30 days and then to the police station to excuse himself from his employ.

Andy thanked the Marshal for his support and handed over the badge. Andy was hoping the Marshal would refuse to take it and proceed to try to talk him into staying. Instead, he took the badge and tossed it unceremoniously into the desk drawer.

"Good Luck, Andy. God Speed...oh, and before I forget. You are most certainly a jackass."

Andy went to the stable, saddled up his horse and led him outside, only to find the Inspector saddled up and waiting.

As they rode slowly to the south, Andy asked if there were any instructions.

"Don't get yourself killed. Get the names of the outlaws. Get out of town and get back here. Marshal knows how to get in touch with me with the information. I suspect there might be a reward for this information, but I don't know for certain."

Andy departed, crossed the river and headed southwest...wondering all the while why he was likely sacrificing so many things to take on the challenge of this ride and investigation.

HARD ON THE TRAIL

It wasn't until mid-afternoon two days out that Andy stopped thinking about Katie and his lapse of judgement.

That shift in rational thought was created by the aches and pains of being in the saddle for so long.

"Should've given some thought to the fact that I haven't been riding as much as I had in previous months," he moaned to the breeze blowing in his face.'

His back and his hind-quarters sent the same message..."you still have eight days in this saddle before you get to Amarillo."

"Eight more days?" he moaned again.

As a drover he was in the saddle and on the trail for weeks at a time. It was a way of life. No. It was just life.

"Someday somebody smarter 'n me will figure out how to come up with a way to deal with distance and time."

Andy grew up with "a day's ride" as a way to tell how far he had come and how long it would take to get there

He knew, after several rides to and from Amarillo, that it was 10 days ride to get there or back. That's assuming of course Mother Nature didn't intervene...or Indians...or a lame horse...or wildfires...of any of a host of other impediments that a person couldn't even imagine.

The route was really a combination of trails...some almost groomed by traffic, others less so and unpredictable in terms of conditions.

He remembered the lessons from his dad. "The shortest distance is a straight line from where you are to where you are going. Get out there and wander about and it will take you more time on the trail. There was a reason all of those fellows before you decided to take that particular trail."

"Wise man, my father."

He turned his thoughts to his horse. His partner on the trail was durable and efficient. He could, of course, be coerced into a trot or canter. If he sensed danger or urgency of any other kind he would gallop, but it wasn't going to last for a long time.

A combination of a walk and some combination of those gaits would usually cover about 30 miles an hour, based on speed measurements used by the railroad engines.

Heading for Amarillo would normally be covered in those 30 miles for every eight hour day. Get there faster riding more than eight hours or by moving up to a faster pace...walks were about four of those miles per hour. A four-beat trot would be about eight miles per hour and a three beat rapid canter, Andy's favorite ride because it was smooth and efficient, would produce about 15 miles per hour. He knew from experience that a gallop would cover ground at about 35 miles per hour, but it required a little extra encouragement. It couldn't be sustained on one horse, especially on hard-scrabble hills, muddy gullies, and heavy sage brush.

So, no matter how he figured it, Andy had eight more days on that saddle, considerably more than he had told Katie that it was going to take. That brought him back to Katie.

"Why did I do this? What made it seem so important? Is she ever going to forgive my thoughtlessness?

AMARILLO

It is certainly a cow town, but without the energy and growth that was in Wichita.

Andy tied up his horse, slapped the dust off his clothing with his hat and went about looking like a drover. First things first, toss down a drink and ask around if anybody was hiring.

During one of his few sane moments, he found himself wondering why he didn't make some effort to say goodbye to Katie.

He desperately needed to come up with a way to justify this foolish adventure...one that could well result in the loss of so many things that were now important to him. Ultimately, it was his bruised ego that reminded him that Katie had actually dismissed him from her presence and she had, indeed, forbade him to talk with her father. Both circumstances were terribly painful and even more so because he knew for a fact that she was right in doing so.

Four hours after arriving in Amarillo, a fellow in better-than-drover clothing walked up to Andy's position at the bar.

"You new in Amarillo?".

"Yup. Passing through. Looking for a hand?"

"No. What I am looking for is somebody who can shoot a rifle and ride a horse at the same time."

"Well, that's easy enough. I was in the cavalry. Good at both of those things."

"If you are as good as you think you are, there's 20 dollars a week for you."

"What am I shooting at?"

"Does it make a difference?"

"Well, yes, as a matter of fact it does."

"No kids. No women. Only guys who are going to be trying to kill you."

"Hell, that sounds like being back in the war down south."

"Almost the exact same thing. In case you're wondering, the fellows that we are shooting at are stealing our cattle and running them."

"Who does the herd belong to?"

"Several ranches and drives, we're just trying to put them back together."

"This sounds like a group of men that I worked with for a while who were rustling cattle and then combining herds. That what this is?

"I guess you could say that."

"Worked well for me last time. I see no problem with it as long as I get paid."

"Ready to ride tomorrow?"

"Where we headed?"

"You'll recognize the country when we get there."

"Who is the trail boss?"

"You got many more questions?"

"I'm funny about wanting to know who I'm working for."

"The Myers brothers from out the other side of Lubbock. They have several ranches out in Colorado and Wyoming territories. Just quit asking questions, show up and do your job. We'll keep you busy if you can do that."

"You payin' me for signing up or do I have to work the first week."

"Why you asking?"

"If you were payin' now, I'd buy you a drink. No silver in my pockets right at this particular time, however. I was heading south when I got here, hoping for a cash deal or a card game. You pay me a bit in advance, and I'll buy the drinks. I'd also like to get a room so I'm ready for tomorrow. Have we a deal?"

"Good idea. I have work to do so I'll collect the drink some other time. Here's some silver against your first pay. Be over at the holding pens at sun-up. There should be eight or nine other guys with us. Clean your firearms. Be ready to ride."

...and with that he was gone. Andy delayed a few minutes, finished his Rye and then headed for his horse.

Perfect situation. I got the information I needed. There is a full moon so there is enough light to ride by tonight. If me and my horse can maintain an efficient trot I'll be plenty far away from Amarillo.

Throughout the night, Andy created a series of scenarios that he might face when he returned to Wichita and Katie. Somewhere around midnight he stopped for some rest that didn't involve the motion of the ride. In his last awake moment, with the moon directly overhead, he decided he could not put any more time and emotional energy into trying to come up with an excuse for what he had done. He would just have to admit the decision was the wrong one and beg her forgiveness. Love can do strange and wonderful things so maybe forgiveness might be possible. For a brief period he wished he could come down with severe cases of amnesia and not know where, and who, he was.... but, instead, he knew he had made a terrible mistake. What he came down with, he reasoned, was a severe case of insanity laced with lunacy.

A DOSE OF REALITY

On the fourth day out Mother Nature decided to make herself known. The wind began howling by midday and the rain began as horizontal sprinkles which quickly became a pelting rain punctuated by frightening lightning bolts coming from way up in the dark, rolling clouds. For what had to be hours, Andy and his horse went deep into the breaks and arroyos to avoid being struck by one of the strikes.

The problem with being down in those washes was the mud...soil down in those places was washed away and the resulting quagmire was smothering and bottomless . The threat was flash floods. Combined, it was necessary to be very cautious about where you were going and at what speed.

In that area there was little shelter... lots of sagebrush and no man-made structures. Andy wasn't sure exactly where he was because the skies were shrouded in angry clouds. He was relatively certain he was somewhere around a little settlement that the locals called "Pampa" because he had been through there several times taking a herd over to the grasslands that lay north and east of there. He had a little shiver when he remembered why herds quit going up there.

This was what the Arapahoe and Cheyenne called sacred ground and their leader, Chief Black Kettle, was a ferocious warrior. Although Andy had heard that the tribes and Black Kettle were working more closely with the US government, he wanted no interaction with any one of them.

By luck and light provided by a bolt of lightning Andy spotted a sandstone overhang on the edge of the butte and he decided to accept the accommodations. Picking his way around the rim, he found a trail down and was soon out of the rain for the first time in many hours. The sandstone overhang created just enough room for Andy and his horse to get out of the elements. The horse soon pushed up against the wall of the shelter, sighed and closed his eyes...sending the message that he was no longer available for work or service.

Not many folks realize that lightning bolts makes many different kinds of noise when it strikes the ground. Knowing that, Andy didn't particularly react to the squeal that resonated from a particularly violently strike that hit on the other side of the arroyo just before he fell asleep.

The rain ceased suddenly just as the sun was going up to the east. The sudden silence woke both man and beast.

Andy's survey of his surroundings produced nothing of significance, but he didn't remember seeing what looked like a couple of outcroppings on the very top of the mesa across the creek. The once dry creek bed was now flowing like a river after the overnight storms. He knew he had to work around to the south before he could go east so they carefully picked their way through the slippery mud to the top of the rim before he mounted, and they were on their way again.

A couple of very slow hours later, they found a place where they could ford the creek. Andy decided to stay astride the horse as equine footing was going to be of value on the hardscrabble bottom of the creek-turned-torrent.

The return to the objects that piqued Andy's curiosity was faster due to the sandstone make-up of the mesa. As he neared the site, he knew this expedition was a bad idea.

The two remains were one horse and one rider, both certainly killed by a lightning strike. They were both burned badly and most certainly never knew what hit them.

Andy walked over to the rider but couldn't make out any detail of the head and shoulders. He slumped to the ground, however, when he noticed the cowboy had a badly deformed left hand with the reins tightly wrapped around his fingers and wrist.

"Lefty, Lefty, Lefty. How could you let this happen?"

"Lefty" Jenkins was a ropin' legend. When he came into this world in Baton Rouge, his mother rejected him due to his left hand and arm. He had but two fingers and a malformed thumb. Both his upper and lower arm had abnormalities that kept him from full movement of the appendage.

Andy had first met Lefty when he came onto a drive headed for Nebraska Territory. Lefty could shoot a rifle with incredible accuracy due to the fact that he was born with a rifle rest. More amazing, however, was that his overused and over-developed right hand and arm allowed him exceptional skills and strength when it came to handling a rope or lariat. He could launch the tether with incredible accuracy, pinning any body part of an animal and he would often take the beast to the ground with one sudden jerk.

Andy knew Lefty well. He knew that Lefty was a believer in his oft-stated philosophy... "Whatever's coming is supposed to be mine." He repeated it all the time, with conviction. He probably said it when he rode out on top of a mesa in the middle of just-passed thunderstorm.

Gathering up Lefty's possessions and tying them on his horse, Andy noticed Lefty's rifle stock had "Amanda" carved into the well-seasoned wood. Andy decided he would ask the former ranger that he was working for to try and deliver the property to the appropriate authority.

Andy left the saddle, bridle and reins on the horse. They had been modified to meet Lefty's physical needs and, frankly, Andy did not want to remove them from the remains of the horse.

Andy piled up some of the larger rocks from the Mesa, creating a cairn that would protect the remains until they would be so unpleasant that nothing would want to defile them.

He went in search of a something that would serve as a headstone but was just about to give up when he spied a peculiar rock that was laying on top of a couple of rounded stones.

Every stone on the mesa looked like river rock...round, smooth and featureless.

He picked up the rugged, jagged and pointed piece and couldn't help but notice that it looked like a fossilized lightning bolt.

"Figures." Andy whispered softly as he bid the final adios to Lefty.

"Lost a couple of days. Should be there early in the morning three days from now...if I'm where I'm thinking I am. Glad the storm has gone on. I have light and a sun to be my beacon."

Almost exactly as he had calculated, Andy arrived in Wichita on his very tired and unhappy horse on the morning of his 10th day. He took the horse to the stable, asked that it be taken care of, and headed off down the street on foot.

First stop was the Marshal. As soon as he stepped in the door, it was clear that he had a problem.

"Can I help you with something, you Jackass?"

"I was hoping that you were hiring and that I could apply for a position."

"Don't have an opening."

"As I understand it, you know how to get in touch with the authorities about the names of a gang rustling livestock and killing drovers. Would you be so kind as to pass along the following: Myers Brothers west of Lubbock with ranches in Colorado and Wyoming."

"I will get the telegram off to him. I'm sure they will appreciate the information."

"I'm surprised to see you. Given what we have heard about the storm, the floods and the wildfires, many of us didn't think you would make it."

"Wildfires? I didn't see any sign of them."

"Likely they were south of you then. Lucky for you. Good day, Jackass."

All of the messages were delivered in the manner they should have been. Andy saw no value in remaining in the office. Next stop, the school.

"I will just have to accept whatever I'm confronted with."

Locked. Nobody there. He headed for the Munger House, approaching it with trepidation.

Locked. Nobody there, either.

Andy made the decision to go over to the Southern, change clothes and clean up. Once he got there it was obvious that he needed to get a couple of acres of trail dust off his body, so he made his way over to O'Hara's Barber Shop for a bath, yes, but also for some direction and a good dose of common sense.

Andy entered the Barber Shop and found O'Hara sitting in his barber chair.

"Well, well. What do we have here. Appears to be a dusty Jackass. Sorry. Don't allow jackasses in the tub."

"Well, OK. No bath. How about sharing some suggestion on how I can ask for forgiveness for my sins and stupid decisions?"

"Fresh out of sympathy, tolerance, and direction. I would suggest you try heading for the bar and drink yourself into a self-indulgent stupor."

"The writing is on the wall...no friends, no understanding and, maybe, only a past here in Wichita."

"I understand. My apologies. To all. Now. I have to find Katie."

Andy started back to the Munger House...haltingly at first but his pace quickened as he got ever closer. He literally and physically threw himself at the door, ending with a crash on the floor in the living room. As he started to get up, he found himself looking into to wide-eyed and startled family....every one of them sitting at the dining room table.

"Andy! Oh my God."

Katie was red-eyed and soaking wet with tears. Mrs. Munger had an expression on her face that made Andy fear for his life. Darius appeared to be calm and collected although clearly concerned about the upheaval that impacted the entire family... but most importantly, eldest daughter Katie.

It was at that time that Andy, for the first time in his life, collapsed to the floor in grief, not knowing what he could do to make amends for his poor judgement. Coupled with physical exhaustion was the potential of losing everything, his self-hatred for hurting Katie and the loss of acceptance and respect from the Mungers. He was further burdened with an overwhelming sense of worthlessness.

His tears, his begging for forgiveness and the extent of his distress combined to shock the Munger family out of their collective emotions. Mrs. Munger, in her role as a mother, crossed the room and sat on the floor, putting her hand on Andy's head. His uncontrolled sobbing began to lessen as she softly spoke to him saying "Andrew, we just don't know what to think of your actions."

Too make the circumstance even more complex, a knock came at the door. Darius responded but made certain he blocked the entry with his body. He then stepped outside but soon returned. He stood there a moment but then delivered the message he had received from Marshal Meagher after his apology for the interruption.

"The inspector would like to thank Andy for solving the murders and theft that has been taking place in Oklahoma and Kansas Territories. The Texas Rangers have been trying to solve the crimes for over a year and Andy did it in a week. His exact words were "The country is forever grateful for your very brave and capable assistance."

While the words did little to solve the greater problems, it did provide something different in terms of human tolerance and understanding.

Katie's expression had softened, and her tears were no longer flowing down her blushed cheeks.

She slowly got up from her chair and took several ever-so-small, hesitant steps until she was standing directly above Andy, who was still lying on the floor rolled up in a ball. He remained incredibly distraught.

"Andrew Graham, why would you be so stupid and childish to do such a thing in that manner. Do you not respect me, my family, and my love for you. You broke my heart and almost broke my spirit. I have told myself, several times, that I will never be able to completely forgive you and your self-indulgent behavior. If I didn't love you so much I would wipe you and your memory out of my mind. GET UP! Be the man I expected you to be. Ask my forgiveness and hold me so I know you are back, and you will never be such a fool again."

Andy began to uncoil and sheepishly looked at the family that he so wanted to be part of.... something he was still afraid he was losing.

"Maybe it is necessary to do something that will allow me to have more control over you. We must talk about our wedding... assuming my father still blesses the union."

Darius was caught off guard by the reference to his blessing. He took a moment to gather his thoughts and then spoke haltingly.

"For the past six days I have been intending to hunt you down for what you did to my daughter... and my family. I found myself both hating you and being sad that you hadn't turned out to be who we thought you were. I am certain that it will take some time before you earn my complete trust, I'm afraid. On the other hand, there is some part of me...and probably the others...that is pleased that you are going to be, once again, part of the Munger Family.

....and with that, Katie collapsed into Andy's arms, sobbing, once again, uncontrollably.

Emotions being what they were, it seemed the best thing to do was to allow the Mungers their privacy and recovery while allowing Andy to return to the Southern for some badly needed rest and mental restoration. He apologized one more time, turned and excused himself as he headed out the door.

Early the next morning, Andy went downstairs to get some breakfast in the just-now-opened dining room of the Southern Hotel. He had just seated himself when Randall, the owner, brought over a written message that was delivered by Marshal Meagher.

"If you're done running all over hell's-half-acres looking for law breakers and putting yourself at risk, it would be a good idea to show up for work today."

With that, breakfast was cancelled, and Andy headed onto the street because he wanted to complete his morning tour on time. As he went past O'Hara's, he heard a loud "Hee-Hawwwww". Andy looked over to the door as O'Hara continued...." you're still a jackass but I'm told you might grow out of it."

Arriving at the police station, Andy developed a sense of dread about going in because he didn't know what he was facing. He knew he had a job again, but he didn't know how he should react.

The Marshal was there, at his desk. Officer Smith was seated on a chair near one of the cells.

"So. Sit down. Give us the story of what happened and how you were able to get that information so fast when the Rangers and a couple hundred other lawmen couldn't do it for more than a year," gushed the Marshal.

Andy spared no detail. The process was healing. He began to understand the depth of the impact on so many people and he swore to himself that he had, finally, grown up.

The inspector said many, many people wanted information about who had solved the case but, wisely, he divulged nothing as there would be many people, over many years, that would probably like to even the score.

They had barely completed the story when the door swung open and in walked Darius Munger with the City Clerk and a couple pounds of paperwork.

"Andy, now that you are back and, it seems, you aren't going to leave again, Katie insists it's time to close the purchase of the Perkins property. Is that all right with you? Katie has already signed the documents."

Following the signings, Andy went in search of Katie.

She was in the school when he got there and she immediately stood upright, seeming almost guarded and apprehensive.

"Katie, I am so, so ashamed and sorry. I was so afraid that I was losing you and your love. Please know that I now know the extent of my feelings for you and the promise of our lives together."

Her hands dropped to her side, and she looked like she was going to begin crying again. She took a deep breath, lifted her hands and extended her arms as he rushed into her hug. Then she abruptly pushed him away.

"I am here to tell you that if you ever do anything even slightly like that again, it will take some very capable lawman, someone such as yourself, to find what remains of you. Do you understand?"

With the next hug the healing began again.

A REQUEST FOR ASSISTANCE

When Andy returned to the office the next morning, he was greeted by the Marshal who clearly was both excited and apprehensive.

"I have received a telegram from the Federal Marshal's Office in our nation's capital. They are inquiring about who it was that broke up a ring of the cattle thieves. They have asked for our assistance at the urging of the Marshal's offices in Kansas City and Joplin."

Andy's first thought was to avoid, at all costs, anything that might create something like what he had just been through.

...but, then, there was his curiosity and the call to duty.

"What would be so important that so many offices would have to be involved?"

Meagher sensed that was going to be the next question.

"Evidently there is a gang of former Confederate soldiers who had fought, and lost, at Mine Creek in '64. They are hanging around the Fort Scott area and are still carrying the war with them. Local law enforcement, such as it is, says that any attempt to calm things down on their part only makes the matter worse. They have been unruly enough to be considered threatening, especially so with the negroes. The Feds want somebody who can speak the language of the soldier, the intent being to fit into their group to find out who the leaders are."

The Marshal closed with a question of which he already knew the answer.

"As I recall, you know that area fairly well. Isn't that right?"

Andy wondered which part of his life he wanted to expose as a basis of response.

"Well, my first 16 years of life were in Fort Scott and I know the countryside very well. However, I would think that much has changed since my departure. The reference to the Mine Creek Battle is interesting to me. While in the Union Army, my company was ordered to be ready to march to the Mine Creek area because of a significant buildup of Confederate troops. It was rumored, at the time, that as many as 7,000 Confederate men were already there and even if we could get there to join the 2,500 Union men already in the area before the fighting broke out, we would only be able to bring our numbers to 4,000 or so."

"We broke camp and headed from Texas and across Oklahoma for Mine Creek in late September, expecting to be in East Central Kansas no later than the second week of October. We began seeing Confederate soldiers, waving white, heading south on October 5th, fleeing on foot, horseback or any other method of conveyance."

"Later, some of the soldiers who felt safely away from the battlefield told us that Union Colonels Frederick Benteen and John Phillips outwitted Confederacy General Sterling Price quickly as they dispatched their troops in a divide-and conquer-maneuver that had the 7,000 men of the Confederacy not knowing where to go, how to fight or when to give up and escape. The 2,500 Union troops were reported to be better equipped, significantly better armed, better trained, and better fed. It was all over very quickly but everybody from both sides said it should be rightfully acknowledged as the largest Civil War Battle to be fought in Kansas."

"I have long wondered why it became the 'Civil War' when it started out as 'The War between the States'. We all know, and God knows too, there was nothing 'civil' about that war. Absolutely nothing...and yet there remains those who are still willing to continue fighting the war."

Marshal Meagher studied Andy's face to make certain his message, and his feelings, were completely understood.

"Marshal, how many of these former soldiers are still in the area and causing trouble?"

"Kansas City says if appears to be thirty or forty of them, quite a few of them being negroes. Many are bivouacked in the general area of Fort Scott, others are in temporary shelters around Pawnee Station but some as far North as near to Topeka and South as far as Parsons," he explained, while using a map of the territory on the wall to give a feel for the scope of the "occupation".

"Are they organized? How do they communicate?"

"From what I hear, they are generally transient and very mobile. They rarely rely on written communication. Seems like they may have determined what worked with the slavery movement of recent years in terms of communicating with people spread over large areas. There is a general opinion that all that needs to be done is to round up whomever is considered as a leader, inform them that the war is over and if they want to get on with their life....without lawmen bird-doggin' them forever...they need to call off their almost-military lifestyle and find something productive to do with the rest of their natural born lives."

Andy was quiet and reflecting on what he had learned in the last few weeks.

"I need to talk with Katie."

"Good idea, Andrew."

THE DECISION

Immediately upon departing the office, Andy spotted Katie walking down the boardwalk from the school.

As they slowly walked toward the Munger House, Katie listened intently to the information that had been provided by the Marshal. Then they stopped walking and she, too, fell silent.

Eventually she let her feelings and emotions loose in a ten-minute dissertation on why she did not want him to go, all the time standing in the same spot at the end of the street, affording them some amount of privacy.

"I see nothing but risk and danger in this assignment."

"Katie, I think that is a fair analysis, given the fact there is a relatively minor amount of information about the leadership and activities of the group."

They had just arrived at the Munger House when Katie suddenly spun around and put her hands on Andy's chest, stopping him in his tracks.

"It is important that we meet with Mother and Father so they will understand we are talking with each other about this. Let me see if they are home."

After what seemed like an eternity, Katie opened the door and asked Andy to come in.

Darius and Mrs. Munger were seated at the table to listen to the appeal... each with a seriously concerned expression on their face.

"How does this discussion vary from your most recent misadventure," asked Darius.

"Right at this time, I don't think there is much difference .....HOWEVER... this time the request is from one of the highest authorities in this country...AND I'm not approaching the task like a bounty hunter, BUT RATHER a lawman carrying out my duties...AND I'm communicating with the ones that I love...AND I can approach the duty tasks in precisely the same manner that I used previously...going in with the anonymity afforded a drover and out with the protection afforded a federally-authorized law enforcement officer", explained Andy, trying to present in a light-hearted manner.

Katie studied Andy's face, took a deep breath and then almost silently exhaled.

"Andy, I am seeing your enthusiasm for this challenge and your sense of professionalism makes me feel much more secure in your approach. I think I can speak for my parents when I say that we do not want to be a burden as you go about your role as a law officer. How long will you be away from Wichita?"

"I am expecting to be on the trail for about a week.

Katie stared into his eyes and declared her love for him.

Darius, deep in thought, whispered "God Speed" as he shook his head, not believing what he had just heard from his daughter.

ON THE HUNT

Andy departed the Southern just before day-break, stopped to saddle his horse and was on the trail with the day's first rays.

He intended to take routes that were known to him as a drover because once you get into the forests of black walnut and pecan in eastern Kansas, it is hard to get around without getting surrounded by the woods and unable to get your bearings.

There were probably five or six relatively direct "trails" to get to Missouri. One of them, the Osage Trail, took him very close to an area known as "the Mounds". Being in this area brought back dark and uneasy memories.

###

During Andy's first two or three years of driving cattle he made a very small number of good friends and a considerably larger number of what could best be called "acquaintances". All were unique in their own way, and all required some degree of anonymity and some measurable amount of unique respect.

Midway through the third summer, Andy met a tall, very thin man with bushy bright red hair and a matching beard. He introduced himself to Andy as "Bones" and Andy immediately assumed it was because was nothing more than skin and bones. Later he would learn that Bones was given the moniker by a long-time friend whose nickname was "Thumbs". Thumbs was so named because his two opposable digits were torn off when his lariat became loop-wrapped around his thumbs just before he and the steer went in opposite directions. Thumbs often told stories about Bones being able to communicate with the dead... especially if he were able to hold a piece of their clothing or, even better, a bone.

Thumbs was once a sea-faring deckhand on steamers plying the Atlantic but came west to change his name, profession, and luck. On two occasions, Thumbs reported that there were those who were missing and presumed dead and, after a brief period of trance-like meditation, Bones was able to ride directly up to their skeletons....one on the open prairie and the other in a hastily dug grave near a small settlement.

After a very difficult drive on the Goodnight-Loving, Bones, Thumb, Andy and a particularly strange newcomer named Bothwell decided to head back toward Louisiana because Thumbs needed to experience the sea again and Bothwell was seeking the services of a psychic or mystic healer. Andy and Bones went along, Andy, because he was needing an escape from the steers while Bones was intrigued with the mention of a psychic, because, obviously, they might be able to explain his ability to communicate with the "un-living".

Their chosen route took them along the Osage Trail and a couple of ramshackle cabins owned by a family named the Benders. They had built these shelters early in the 1870s and named their lodges "The Wayside Inn".

One of the Benders was daughter Kate. Calling her eccentric was a gross understatement. She often introduced herself as "Professor Miss Kate Bender"... a psychic and mystic of considerable powers. She was also quite buxom.

The four drovers stopped at the inn. Accommodations were spartan as the little cabin was "divided" into two sections... meaning a sheet of fabric pulled across the main room of the structure. Guests were always directed to sit at the dining table, two with their backs to the sheet and two to the outside wall.

On the night in question, Bothwell and Bones both set with their backs to the fabric, Andy and Thumbs on the wooden wall.

Kate and her younger brother John Junior came into the room to provide service to the visitors. Kate was wearing a very low-cut blouse, causing Bothwell to declare, quite loudly, "I'll be damned if there ain't more than two or three acres to that chest." John Junior, who exhibited several characteristics of being a bit slow, took exception to the comment and started to move toward Bothwell.

With very little physical movement and within the blink of an eye, Bothwell's 45's were in his hands and there was the tip of a gun barrel on each of John Junior's eyelids. The speed of the draw caught everybody off-guard. Andy was the first to speak, saying it would probably be best if all concerned would use better manners and noted that the four guests were very tired from many days on the trails. The tension eased a bit. Nobody apologized. Nothing more was said for a few minutes.

When the Benders departed the cabin, Andy commented that he hadn't seen anybody that could draw that fast, even with all of his travels.

"My right is faster than my left.... that's why there is six notches on my right grip and only five on my left." Andy let that settle in and did what he could to help his friends relax. Food was served and each finished their serving...to say they "enjoyed" it would be an exaggeration, "tolerated" it was probably more accurate.

Bothwell was the only person still at the table as the other three found their way to cots in which to sleep. Bothwell had produced a couple of silver coins and purchased the remainder of a bottle of Rye and while everybody went to sleep, he was sitting there drinking while wishing he had something more than a not-quite-taut curtain to lean on.

Come morning, Bothwell and Kate were nowhere to be found and Bothwell's horse was not at the rail.

After a certain amount of discussion, Bones, Thumbs and Andy decided to head on to the south, expecting to catch up with Bothwell.

They also decided that if Bothwell didn't show up after a day's ride and a night's sleep, they would return to the Wayside Inn to find out where he might be.

Round about midnight, under a full moon, Bothwell's horse arrived without anybody in the saddle. The three riders arrived at the Wayside Inn just after daybreak and they hailed the cabin with a "Hey, Benders, Halloo!" Both John's were the first to awaken, then Mrs. Bender and, finally, Kate, the Professor, herself.

After inquiries, accusations and innuendos, John Junior proclaimed that Bothwell finally drank himself into a stupor and fell to the floor, hitting his head in the process. John Junior then reported that he got Bothwell on his feet and put him on his horse, ordering him not to return. That, he said, was the last he had seen of Bothwell.

Thumbs and Andy asked for, and received, permission to search the property, which didn't take long.

Satisfied that Bothwell wasn't there and with nothing seeming amiss, the three mounted up and rode on to the south, with Bothwell's horse trailing behind.

About a mile down the trail, Bones abruptly reined in his horse, dismounted, sat down on a fallen Cottonwood tree trunk with his head in his hands and his hands over his ears... saying "something is wrong. Bothwell is talking to me. He's saying things that I can't understand but he is screaming and shouting".

Thumbs turned his head and cocked one eyebrow.

"Did you see the notches on the grips of John Junior's Colts... eleven notches on 'em just like Bothwell's and they looked a lot like his too."

Andy said quietly, "Let's put some distance between us and the Wayside Inn while we figure out what to do."

Once the trio arrived in Oswego, they sought out Marshal Tall Man, an Osage half-breed that served as the only lawman in the region. They told him their story and he said he often heard about disappearances of travelers and settlers in that area but there was little he could do except drop in when he was in the area...and that was infrequently.

They surrendered Bothwell's horse to the Marshal after deciding to continue their trek to Louisiana.

MYSTERIES SOLVED

Two or three years later, as a drover returning to the herds, Andy found himself a couple of miles from the Wayside Inn and rode over to find the property had been demolished, burned, and abandoned.

After a couple of inquiries to some of those living in the woods around the area, Andy was told stories that assaulted his senses, and he was shaken by horror and disgust.

He learned the Benders often killed visitors by hitting them in the back of the head with a hammer through the curtain and then dropping the bodies into a cellar under the kitchen....disposing of them by burying the victims after dark.

Guests who were known to have money, which would have included Bothwell, who had a habit of jingling coins in his pockets, were most often targeted. Other times visitors had their throats cut while sleeping. One was even a little girl who was evidently traveling with her father.

A search was performed by the family of Dr. William York of Independence and 21 bodies were found on the prairies surrounding the Wayside Inn. There were reports that those searching were often assisted by a strange man who wandered the countryside, and he would often be able to tell the authorities where the burial sites were. Some of the folks familiar with the searches said the red-headed drifter often said he had conversations with the dead to determine where they were interred.

Andy hadn't returned to the area for quite some time and for good reason...it was a difficult story, true, but he often felt guilty that he had not done something that might have saved lives of others after his experience at "the Mounds".

RETURNING TO THE HUNT

Andy easily found his way to Fort Scott even though he hadn't been in the town for many years. He was, once again, excited to see the Fort, which was being well taken care of by the towns-folk, even though it had been closed as a military installation back in 1855.

Very little had changed on the grounds of the fort, but things were certainly different in the city. After the Civil War, Fort Scott was in direct competition with Kansas City in regards to attracting the businesses, manufacturers and the offices of the various railway systems. Significant growth was seen in all business sectors. The growth changed the city in many ways, one of which was the way the existence of Fort Scott was viewed by the population. The conflicts created by issues related to slavery complicated life for many Fort Scott citizens. It remained squarely in the camp of "Bleeding Kansas" and the final free-for-all that resulted in Kansas coming into the Union as a Slave-Free state. There remained a measurable amount of sensitivity about the negroes, even though several companies of Black Officers had proven themselves while fighting in the Civil War. Many of them committed to provide unofficial law enforcement support after the war.

It was one of those officers who Andy would try to contact to get as much information as he could about the renegades. During one of those scouting sessions, Andy was approached by an attorney who identified himself as J.B. Johnson. Johnson was quick to report that he was in touch with law enforcement, such as it was.

Johnson explained that while there had not yet been incidents that created loss-of-life, the mood and movement of the former soldiers often created anxiety within the townsfolks. There was a long-standing and growing concern that they might get themselves organized and become more aggressive in their actions.

Johnson, too, was of the opinion that there were only four or five men in the group with enough power to keep everybody together. They were truly a rag-tag band and would most likely yield to pressure applied through their group of "leaders", especially if one former officer named Bass Reeves was involved.

Andy asked if he knew any others that might be one of the leaders. Johnson said he had an opinion, but it would need review by others to make certain. Andy followed up by asking who else he should be talking to.

Johnson reached into his breast pocket and produced a very substantial list of those who should be interviewed. Andy could immediately see that using this approach was going to amount to several weeks of work. He also knew that if he were active in the area for that long, virtually everybody would know who he was and what he was up to.

As a result of all those factors, Andy decided to make some inquiries directly to some of those who might appear to be involved with the group. He soon found himself on the streets, talking to anyone who was wearing former military clothing.

Andy quickly determined that his most effective conversation-starter involved getting into a discussion that included a brief summary of his war experience. He would then change the subject to how the only thing he could do for work after the war was to herd cattle. He would increasingly raise his voice just a bit while saying he wanted something more than that and that he was looking for other men who were troubled by the lack of options. He soon found that he was a participant in a very informal organization, the constituents being troubled with similar discontent.

After one of those conversations Andy was approached by an exceptionally tall and ruggedly built negro fellow who was often wearing what little was left of a Confederate Officer's topcoat.

"Seems as you are pickin' through the rubble of the war. So, what's your interest and, even more importantly, what's your intent?"

Andy intentionally delayed his response, attempting to match the intensity of the inquiry.

"Can't seem to come up with a way to find employment appropriate to my skills and I expect others are sharing that same frustration."

"You think this motley little group of riffraff has answers to that situation?"

"Hope so. I been askin' and listening for so long that I figure I know about everything there is to know about our circumstance but there just isn't an answer that presents itself. Some of these gentlemen are of the mind that the solution might be lawlessness. That don't seem like a good idea to me."

"Over the years I have learned that many times being hungry and cold makes one feel like some of that money that other people have should be spread around a little better than it seems to be. That is particularly true to most of my race."

"I believe that premise to be true. Also true, however, is the fact that taking other peoples' money and belongings will certainly put one on the wrong side of the law and doesn't tend to make one have friends either. I can speak with some degree of knowledge about being sought by law enforcement. Having to lay low isn't any way to go through life."

"Name's Reeves, Bass Reeves. Yours?"

"Not important...besides, I used so many names I'm not sure I can say for certain who I am."

"OK by me."

"How many gentlemen are here that would work if there was work to be done?"

"They get paid for doin' that work?"

"That would be the intent."

"Probably somewhere in the 25 or 30 range."

"What skills do we possess?"

"Soldier things. You know. Ride, shoot, fight."

"Everybody that survived the War Between the States can do those things. Some better than others. We need to find those who need our skills. We have to deliver the message that we can be and do what somebody needs. We just don't know who and what is on that list."

"There is maybe as many as 50 all told. I tend to underestimate the number of negros. Reckoning by most people is that one out of every four men in our little band is a nigger. That's probably right as that would be about the same as the make-up of the Confederate companies at the end of the fightin'. Now, it's important that while we are making up our lists of the things we need, let's include some honor and pride. Rare commodities right now. Most of us were on the losing side. It's really hard on a man to think about failure day-in and day-out."

"Well-noted and very-well-said, Reeves. I have been planning on getting on the trail tomorrow to see if I can find a herd heading somewhere that I might sign on with. I'm missing being on the move. I need some time to think about this dilemma...and pushing steers will give me that time."

"I have enjoyed...and benefited... from our conversation, Mister No-name."

"As have I, Reeves. I'm of the opinion that you carry some amount of weight with most of these men. Your understanding, thinking and presence clearly comes from your leadership experience as an officer."

"Don't let this tattered garment mislead you."

"A man with your body structure would have had to get that coat especially made...the military doesn't do that for rank-and-file soldiers."

"Well considered and thought out, Mister No-name."

"Please allow me to do some work on behalf of all of us here in this situation. I have a number of people that I can talk to that might be able to come up with answers to these vexing questions. It would be of incredible importance to keep things calm as you can while we work on this."

"I can do that. Please accept my....and my associates'... thanks for being interested in our plight in general and the additional challenges for the niggers. I'm workin' on getting my head and thinking to talk about "negros" but I'm finding the change to be hard since that was what I heard the very first time I heard a human voice."

Andy had no idea what or how to be of assistance, but he knew he would have to find, or create, an opportunity somehow. Everything was growing and changing, he would just have to feel his way around the folds and seams of each of the boxes until he found something worth opening.

He didn't wait until morning to saddle up his horse and head west. He knew somehow the solution was to be found in the energy and growth that was available in Wichita.

With the exception of a couple of hours of not-quite-asleep rest while lying on a grass-covered knoll with his saddle bags as pillows, Andy stayed in the saddle, arriving on the outskirts of Wichita just about the same time that the sun made its appearance.

His timing wasn't convenient as everybody that he needed to see immediately were not yet into the day. He tied up his horse at the stable and walked, slowly and stiffly, to the Southern, hoping that the innkeeper had made good on his promise to finish the bath facilities for his residents and guests.

"Well, good morning to you, Officer Graham, appears you are just off the trail. Might I interest you in the use of one of our bathing facilities?" he said, already at full stride down the hall toward the new building at the rear of the Southern. Andy knew he would already be out of earshot, but he responded with, "yes, please" as a courtesy.

Andy gathered up his lawman's garb, returned to the lobby, made his way down the hall and into the first of three baths. He was looking forward to his return to his Wichita life and its many benefits.... among them comfort, salary....and, of course, Katie.

As he finished getting dressed, he caught sight of his image in the new mirror. "Not bad. Not quite shiny but certainly not bad" he said quietly.

Andrew reported to Marshal Meagher as he should. The discussion was lengthy and the questions many. The Marshal set about writing up a report that would be sent along to the federal offices in Kansas City and Joplin. The only thing that was missing in the report was the plan to remedy the situation and Andy was almost certain that he needed to talk with Darius Munger about the problem. Mr. Munger was intelligent and aware of how things were changing, regardless of how fast they were doing so.

At this time of day, Darius would almost certainly be in his office and Katie was almost certainly putting the final touches on her wardrobe for the day. Andy headed the three blocks down to Mr. Munger's office building.

"Good morning, Sir."

"Well, good morning to you, Andrew. It's good to see you home again. I trust your journey was productive."

"Indeed, it was, Sir. Unfortunately, the learning hasn't produced the solution, just yet. I would appreciate the opportunity to discuss an interesting and complex situation that exists in the Fort Scott area."

Darius took his pocket watch from his vest pocket, opened it up and gave it some consideration before responding to the request.

"I would welcome the opportunity but there are some pressing issues here too. I have been asked to meet with representatives of a transportation company. A fellow by the name of William Fargo and a couple of his partners in the Overland Mail Company want to expand their twice a week routing between Tipton, Missouri and San Francisco. They have developed quite a long list of places they want to service with both mail and conveyance. They tell a good story and a group of us here want to keep track of what they are doing and learn what their plans are. You are most certainly welcome to come along and participate if you would like and if you have the time. I'm sure the Marshal will be attending too."

For a brief moment Andy thought about his wish to see Katie but he also knew she would likely be busy with school matters. He also heard the urgency in Darius' voice and saw it as an opportunity to learn about the things that must happen for the future.

"I appreciate the offer and I would truly like to be in attendance."

"Excellent. Alright then, let's set about getting over to the new school district meeting hall."

OPPORTUNITIES ABOUND.

Over the course of the next three hours, Andy Graham became intensely educated in transportation advancements. Yes, he knew that the railroads had a profound impact on how the country worked and moved but there was a substantial need for more. All considerations had challenges that had to be addressed. There was an urgent need to expand services, schedules, speed, safety, and security.

Overland had created the first transcontinental stagecoach line. It was first the brainchild of two entrepreneurs, Misters Abbot and Downing. Their downfall was their failure to understand the scope and breadth of North America. There was also an ill-fated effort to bring the Overland into a partnership with the Butterfield Stage system, but it never worked as planned.

A few years back, Wells Fargo came into existence. The had established a few routes that allowed for people and commerce to be transported between cities that were not serviced by the railroads. With proven success for most of their routes, in 1867 they ordered 30 Concord Coaches to allow for immediate expansion of routes and services.

The presentation started out as a request to allow the Overland to build a new station so they could initiate service to the surrounding towns. The meeting became, however, a solicitation for investors to assist in paying for the expansion plan. Darius stood up, gazed out the window and then turned to the presenters.

"All of this is well and good but what I am not hearing are the negatives...the shortcomings and failures. There most certainly must be some. What are they?"

An uneasy silence settled over the room.

Mr. Fargo surveyed his partners and, not seeing anybody willing to respond, he stood up and gathered his thoughts.

"Our success has created our greatest problem...security. We first initiated the creation of a banking system that would allow for multiple banking services. We were buying gold, selling paper bank drafts backed by gold and then determined we needed to provide express delivery of gold and anything else of value. The discovery of gold in California and Colorado created immediate markets for our services and transportation systems...primarily train routes."

"We find ourselves woefully deficient in our ability to protect the goods we are shipping. We have not been able to create a means by which we can secure the services of adequate numbers of trustworthy, trained men to ride along with our shipments to protect them from theft."

"We experienced two armed robberies last month in our system. There is no doubt that number will be increasing. Our last estimation of the frequency of these incidents leads us to believe that some 300 robberies and high-jackings will take place over the next 10 years."

"Pilfered paper we can follow through emerging companies like the Pinkerton Detective Agency but once gold is stolen, it becomes untraceable. There are any number of crooks, thieves, and ne'er-do-wells out there and, quite frankly, we haven't found a good way to find, hire and retain quality security men."

The words gob-smacked Andy to the point that he jerked upright... almost falling from his chair and, at the same time, attracting attention from many of those attending. He recognized this was an opportunity...but he also recognized that there was no time in which to plan the content. Throwing caution to the wind, he simply started speaking.

"I am Andrew Graham. I serve as a law enforcement officer here in Wichita. I grew up in a military institution and have a military background. I understand the process of creating well-trained and trustworthy personnel. I have just returned from completing a survey in Fort Scott where trained, experienced men...former white and negro soldiers from both sides...are not only available but they are almost desperately needing the opportunity to

work and become of value to this country once
again."

He stopped for a moment to consider the risk of
making the next statement.

"It is my opinion that upwards of 50 able-bodied
men could be hired and trained to serve as very
capable security personnel for your coaches and
trains. I am also of the opinion that if they were
appropriately attired in something that identifies
them as members of an elite security unit, they
would serve to demonstrate that both Wells Fargo
and Overland clearly understand the need to protect their customers assets."

With that Andy sat back down in the last row
of new chairs and set about wondering if he had
overstepped his boundaries with the just-finished
dissertation.

Mr. Fargo focused on Andy for what was becoming an embarrassing amount of time. He lowered his
gaze until he was able to study Andy over the top of
his spectacles.

"Mr. Graham, are you of the opinion, then, that an
organization can be built and staffed to adequately
provide quality security on an on-going basis."

"Yes, Sir, I am."

"Are you willing to assist us in the effort to do so?"

"With consideration of my already existing commitments."

"Your concept is interesting and somewhat com-
pelling as it addresses a major obstacle for our
growth and our future...and, it sounds as if this

process could be initiated in the very near future, is that correct?"

"In my estimation, yes. Almost immediately. The fact is that it needs to be immediate...for a number of reasons."

"My partners and I need to discuss this strategy. Who would you consider to be able to pull all of this together if we decide to go forward?"

"I would recommend Colonel Bass Reeves. He is a formidable figure with excellent leadership skills...a former Confederate officer who knows virtually every soul in the region...those reputable, as well as those not so."

"What should the pay be for recruits?"

"Sir, I'm afraid I'm don't have enough recent experience to take a position on that. I would encourage you to make certain the initial offer is not too low. These men want to be productive and feel necessary. Please consider a fair wage."

"We will certainly take that under consideration."

"....and please seek out somebody that can design and produce a uniform for your charges. I recommend a striking design with some vivid colors. These men have had enough of the blue and gray...and, of course, the clothing should also be something that allows mobility and comfort during the course of all seasons."

"Perhaps we should contract with you to take care of the many details."

"Perhaps."

THE NEXT STEP.

Following the adjournment of the meeting, Andy had brief conversations with all three of the Overland partners and promised that he would assist in mobilizing the group if they made the decision to proceed. Mr. Fargo said the decision would be made with a sense of urgency and then closed with "we'll put the funding for this in place immediately".

With their departure, Andy took a moment to think about that closing comment.

As the Overland Coach and four outriders departed Wichita, Andy felt a slender hand slip into his. She spun him around and before he could say anything, Katie gave him a crushing, and sustained, hug.

"Andrew, I didn't know you were back."

"Sorry. It has been a very busy day so far."

"Yes, I've heard. Father is about to burst the seams on his vest. He is so excited about the potential and so proud of your leadership."

"You are so beautiful...".

"Now stop that...we're in a public setting."

"I've missed you so very much."

"You were only gone for four days."

"Seems like years."

"Now THAT would get you in trouble."

"I don't want to do that again....."

"Hush."

"I understand."

...and then she was gone as three members of the school board had just arrived to discuss how the new meeting room had functioned during its first event.

Andy walked up the street toward the Marshal's office, hoping he would be there to discuss the just completed proceedings.

As he swung the door open, he jerked to a halt because there simply wasn't any place to stand, let alone sit. City leaders, several visiting railroad executives and more than a few local businessmen were all talking at once. The clamor was deafening, and Darius had to elevate his voice to bring some order to the room.

"Gentlemen, clearly we are all excited about what we heard today. I think the challenge is how to make the strategy benefit Wichita and we will have to address that in the near future. I am of the opinion that the Overland group liked what they heard from Officer Graham and, further, they believe in the strategy being proposed. I would expect the company to focus on trying to put the operation either in, or close to, Kansas City. We need put a proposal in front of them that brings them here."

Marshal Meagher put both of his hands in the air to signal his intent to speak.

"From where I'm sitting.... right here in MY office...it appears that we will have to await communication from the gentlemen from Overland before we can do anything more so, get out...so I can get some work done."

While it was far from orderly, the crowd began to make their way to the door and soon the crowd was reduced to three...the Marshal, Darius and Andy.

"Well, Andrew. That was quite a presentation. Where did the plan come from that allowed you to make such a dynamic proposal?"

"The time that I spent in conversations with men in the Fort Scott area gave me a great amount of insight into their situation. With all of the very important things that are happening in this country, there remains a group of men that possess the skills to do some great things, but they haven't the opportunity to do so. During my hours on the trail I continued to mull over their comments and recall the desperate expressions on their faces."

Darius sat down on the rickety old bench that served many purposes in the Marshal's office.

"Do you feel these men can be trusted? Are they coming to the point that they may start making bad decisions out of frustration and desperation?"

Andy thought about the legitimacy of the inquiry for a few moments.

"I'm afraid there are some that are on the verge of rebellion....some because of the seeming futility of their circumstance and some just because they have led less-than-honorable lives previously. Those lines of work that might become attractive again since they have no work, no food and no money."

The Marshal had been studying Andy's intensity and thought it time to investigate why Andy was so wrapped up in the matter.

"There are many who would say to you 'mind to your own matters'. To me, however, it seems that you have discovered a solution to a couple of problems that most of us would probably not notice or not even know about. That's one thing that makes you both a good lawman and a valuable asset to this city. It does come, unfortunately, with some swamp land...recruiting, training, arming, evaluating...all things that call for skills that most of us don't possess. Any ideas on that?"

"I would be relying on my experiences growing up in the Army and serving similar roles in parts of my adult life."

The Marshal interrupted. "And that's another issue. Am I about to lose my best employee?"

"I don't think anybody is ready to talk about things like that. I'm just going to keep the situation on my mind and see how it grows. These, I think, are very complicated matters on their own...but they are all related, as I see it."

"I would agree with all of that," said Darius, while pulling his pocket watch. "We are very close to being late for dinner...and I have no desire to do battle with the women of the house. It would be wise for us to head that way."

Dinner came about on time and with a great deal of excited conversation. Andy shared more information about his discoveries and his concern was well reflected in his reports and observations. Mrs. Munger and Katie both made intriguing comments during the far-reaching storytelling.

"I'm afraid our lives have come to be surrounded by what is going on in Wichita and we forget, sometimes, that there are many, many stories in the rest of Kansas...let alone the greater world," Mrs. Munger quietly lamented.

"Mother, your knowledge of the world reflects your great powers of observation, and your reading has allowed you insight into matters most people, especially women, would have no awareness of."

Mrs. Munger thought about that for a moment and then agreed. "That's why it is so important that we continue to build an outstanding school system. Knowledge ...ALL knowledge... has value that knows no end. Your profession will have a profound impact on everyone who takes advantage of education being available here."

Darius had been listening to the intensity of the various conversations but felt the need to change the subject.

"I remain concerned about the make-up of these men in Fort Scott. I would like to know more about them. If this goes forward, we will have to evaluate the character of these gentlemen quickly and thoroughly. It will be necessary to re-establish the manner and characteristics that were essential to their military careers. Are they capable of returning to that level of function in short order?"

"There remains a number of concerns in that regard. Colonel Reeves has the ability to communicate with almost anybody. He is introspective, intense and is seen as a leader. There are those, however, that should be scrutinized more thoroughly. One of the men I talked with has small, dark, beady eyes. My father advised, many years ago, that this trait should always be cause for concern. There is this man, a fellow named Jessie James, who has been talking about organizing some of the men into something of a company. I think his intent is to build a small army for purposes of robbery, theft, and other ill-conceived notions. Colonel Reeves observed the same things. This man James is not one of the men I would approach for involvement."

The excitement of the day and the intensity of the evening's discussions brought the energy levels down to the point that the day was about done.

Andy asked Katie if she would like to retire to the parlor for tea. Darius and Mrs. Munger understood the invitation did not include them and they announced their intent to retire for the evening.

While warming the remainder of the day's teapot, Katie turned from the stove and stared intently at Andy, who was aware of her gaze and was wondering what she was about to say.

"You are wanting to put this idea into a working force, aren't you."

"Yes. I do. I think it is important for so many reasons. So, yes."

"How do you do it?"

"I have no real idea on how."

"Would you leave your position with the Police Department?"

"I would hope that Marshal Meagher would allow me a deputy's position similar to what I saw in Fort Scott. There would be value, I believe, in being a lawman...".

"...or it could make you a target."

"Yes. I suppose that is possible."

The room was now quite dark, and their emotions required that they stray from the subject of business to take on the complexities of the many personal issues between the two. They had much to talk about and, indeed, they did so for the next several hours.

NEXT STEP

Andy was awake before the sun climbed to the horizon. He had a fitful night, energized by the concepts of the previous couple of days. Worse yet, the evolving challenges created new ideas. Ideas that dictated the need for new solutions and new opportunities which created new obstacles to overcome.

Following breakfast at The Southern, Andy walked over to the Wichita Mercantile to seek out some expertise in haberdashery, clothing function and fashion.

"Daniel, it is always good to find you here in the store."

"Officer Graham, I could say the same to you."

"I come asking guidance."

"In what regard?"

"Uniforms. Bold designs and colors."

"For whom?"

"A security police force which is not yet formed."

"Interesting...and quite timely."

"Why is that?"

"I have been studying the circulars that have been coming in with what is now almost daily shipments. It seems that companies are moving, relatively quickly, toward putting their employees in clothing that has a uniform look."

"What I am looking for is something that will wear well. It will need to identify the force and be something that people will remember. It must allow for comfort during travel and activity."

"Quite the challenge."

"I know. Oh, yes, the need may be almost immediate."

"In the last month or so we have been approached by two companies that are intending to move to Wichita and enter the clothing manufacturing business. One is a Kansas City, Missouri company with several generations of their family involved. I remember the name because it is spelled a bit differently than expected...Woolf Brothers. The other is a company that we order pocket watches and other personal accessories through. They want to expand to clothing...company with the name of Weckworth."

"If this all comes together, our order could be very large. Upwards of fifty uniforms to start, I'm thinking."

"Yes, well, that would be very nice for them. They intend to provide design suggestions too, as I recall. On the other hand, I would like to present some ideas to you as I have been learning clothing design and assembly."

"Daniel, that would be a wonderful idea. I will need a couple of days to put somethings in place and I'll talk with you about it as soon as I know something of substance."

"Thank you for coming to the Wichita Mercantile. Oh, by the way, I am now Assistant Manager Daniel."

"Another smart choice by ownership. Congratulations, Assistant Manager Daniel."

CHARGE AHEAD

Andy's head was now fully packed with details and burdened with formative overload. His journey down the street to the Marshal's Office allowed him to further put together elements of a strategy for development...so much so that he walked right past the office and didn't realize his detour until he was two blocks past. He turned back in haste.

"Morning, Marshal."

"Good morning, Andrew. There is someone seeking you out. When they learned you weren't on-duty yet they headed for City Hall, saying they would be back shortly."

"Anybody I know?"

"I think he was one of the outriders that was attending to the Overland Coach yesterday. Not sure... but I think so."

"Interesting."

"Yes, I thought so too."

"Hear anything about some clothing companies thinking about moving to Wichita?"

"Two, three months ago but not much since."

"Hmmm."

"Looking for a seamstress?"

"I wish it were that simple."

The Marshal was looking out the window, squinting...and then leaned forward for a better look.

"Seems like your visitor is returning."

"Good. Let's find out what this is all about."

The visitor came into the office as if here were on a mission...and clearly he was.

"Andrew Graham?"

"Yes, I am."

"My name is Allen Forseth. I am associated with the Overland Stage Company, soon to be the Wells Fargo Banking and Transportation Company."

"Interesting. How can I help you."

"I have been asked to advise you that your recommendations have been accepted by ownership and they ask that you do whatever is necessary to move forward with the plan."

"What 'plan'"?

"I was not advised in that regard. Mr. Fargo asked that I tell you that the funding for the project is secure and the company attorneys will arrive in the near future to work out the details of the new security company."

"What 'new security company'"?

"Again, I don't have that information. He also asks that you make the necessary inquiries in Fort Scott to determine the availability of personnel for the company."

"What 'personnel'"?

"I'm afraid this common refrain could become tiresome. I don't know."

"Fortunately, I have just enough information to start this process, but I would certainly like to know to what extent I can make decisions."

"Mr. Fargo said you knew what had to happen, when it had to happen and how it was to happen."

"Please advise Mr. Fargo that I will be making decisions that I believe to be correct, however I am of the opinion that he needs to establish some guidelines to pass along. Until I receive those guidelines, I will assume that I have the right to make decisions that I believe are in the best interests of his company."

"It is my impression that is exactly what he wanted to hear."

"Mr. Forseth, I have much to do and I'm sure you have to head back to Kansas City as soon as possible. Thank you for your assistance and the message."

"Abilene, actually."

"Pardon me?"

"Abilene is where I am headed. Abilene, Kansas...not Texas. I'm getting on a train there to see what options exist for the main office of the new company."

"Please tell Mr. Fargo that Wichita is the right place for the new company."

"It sounds like they are of the opinion that there will be a significant presence in Wichita, particularly since you will likely be living here with your new bride."

"Wait. Where did that information come from?"

"I can't say that I know how Mr. Fargo came to have that information."

"You can't say, or you don't know"?

"Exactly. I'm sure you understand."

"Yes, I think I do."

"Good day, Mr. Graham."

"Safe travels, Mr. Forseth."

STUNNED

Andy stood in the middle of the Marshal's Office, wondering what had just transpired.

Marshal Meagher joined him in trying to make sense of the proceedings.

"I'm not sure what I am...but I'm something that means I have a lot of work to do."

The Marshal shook his head and muttered, to no one in particular, "see, I knew I was going to lose my best employee."

Andy immediately went seeking anybody whose last name was Munger.

It was Mr. Darius Munger, as it turned out. At full stride, almost a sprint. He yelled to Andy from a block away. He was obviously in a very excited state.

"What? What did he want? What did he tell you?"

"In brief. The company is funded. I'm to find personnel. I'm to make any decision that I think needs to be made. They will have offices here in Wichita. I'm getting married. Oh. You know that."

"That is incredible. When?"

"The marriage or the new company? When? Now. Ten minutes ago. Got to get organized. No. Got to find Katie."

Darius took a deep breath. "Yes. Yes, you do."

...and with that Andy headed for the schoolhouse while Darius headed for the Munger House.

SLOW DOWN

Andy cleared the stairs with one long stride and the porch with the next, trying to keep from tearing the door off the hinges. His abrupt, crashing arrival startled students and teacher alike.

"Andrew! What in the world? Students, this is Andrew Graham. He's my best friend and he didn't mean to frighten us...did you Andrew?"

"No. Certainly not. I'm sorry. So sorry.

"What are you so excited about?"

"The company is here. To Wichita! We're bringing it to here...you and I."

"Andy, please be at greater peace. I don't understand. What are you saying."

"They have approved the plan for Overland...I mean, Wells Fargo."

"I think it is best that we talk about this later today, Andrew. This is too much disruption right now."

Andy nodded his head slowly while trying to assemble some sense of order.

"Yes. Right. Certainly."

With that he hurried to Katie, grabbed her around her waist and kissed her as passionately as he ever had, much to the delight of the student body.

Katie was flustered. Excited, embarrassed, flushed and dealing with an unkempt mind right at that moment.

"ANDREW GRAHAM...What are you thinking?

"How much I love you and how excited I am to be marrying you".

The gasps, twitters and giggles were immediately audible, once again.

"...and I feel the same about you Andrew...now begone. You...We...have created enough turmoil and gossip for this day."

Andy almost appeared to float out of the building...certainly so as compared to how he entered it.

NOTICE TO MARSHAL MEAGHE

Andy hurried to the Marshal's Office and arrived with a great deal of excitement and was almost mid-sentence when he stopped, started, and then stopped and started again.

"Marshal, I am finally beginning to get control of my emotions now so I will attempt to pass along what I have learned."

"Already know most of it."

"How.......?"

The Marshal held a just-delivered telegram up in the air passed it back and forth between his hands before giving it to Andy. Andy read it, turned it over to see if there was anything on the reverse. Finding nothing he turned it back over and read it again.

"Mr. Graham: As the new branch manager of our developing business in Wichita, Kansas you are hereby authorized to carry out all of the duties of your position. Please keep me advised of your progress and challenges as you go forward. Ownership agrees to pay you $100 per month for the time being and then will adjust higher with our first branch meeting. We trust that you will practice good judgement and perform your fiduciary duties appropriately. We project the need for 50-70 well trained, well-outfitted and orderly security police in 60-90 days. Please advise, at your earliest convenience, as to where the banking arrangements should be made. We believe in you and your capabilities. Congratulations on your new position. - William Fargo with Henry Wells' participation."

Andy was, once again, completely, and appropriately, stunned.

"...new branch manager of our developing business...congratulations on your new position...?

Andy stared at Marshal Meagher and then uttered "but I already have a position. Don't I?"

The Marshal walked slowly to his desk, sat down in the old squeaky oak chair and leaned back to think. Having gathered his thoughts, he turned the chair to face Andy.

"Well, from where I sit you don't really have any choices to make. If you don't seize on this opportunity, you will be required to return to your previous role as the biggest jackass in Wichita. You would be turning your back on your future wife, her family, the City of Wichita, Kansas, hundreds of desperate men and two of the most powerful industrial leaders in this great country. Any thoughts on any of that?"

Andy's head was spinning. Right up to this very significant point in time he hadn't given any attention to most of those things beyond Katie and her family.

"Yes. Of course. You are right...but I need your help in making this work."

"and that help would be what"?

"Allow me to remain a deputy in the Wichita Police Department."

"Why on earth?"

"Having that position and that badge would, I think, strengthen my position many times as I go about my duties."

"Why do you think that?

"I am going to be working, initially, with 'gentlemen' who have had little experience in industry. Further, most of them will have a history..of one type or another...with law enforcement, most of it negative...but they do respect it, each to one degree or another."

"That shiny badge also makes a good target, however."

"I understand. I intend to keep the badge in my pocket most times."

Meagher dropped his chin to his chest and fell silent. After several moments he exhaled a long whispery "Well.........".

"Since you will be doing work that involves and benefits the city of Wichita, I can see no reason why it isn't possible to retain your commission. We will, however, need to review the situation periodically... and since you are getting such an increase in salary in your new position, there won't be any pay from the city. What do you think?"

"I have absolutely no problem with that proposal. Thank you for your support."

"Least I can do."

KATIE'S UNDERSTANDING

Andy expected that Katie would just be starting classes at the school. Unfortunately, he just couldn't wait until after school to talk with her...even though he knew that should be the plan.

He found himself at the door of the school again. He quietly opened the door to find that, yes, class had begun but Katie was not the teacher.

Andy inquired about her absence and the educator-in-training said that Katie had a meeting in her father's office and would return in approximately an hour. Andy thanked the young gentleman and excused himself. Judging by the smiles of the faces of the students, many hadn't forgotten about the intimate scenes from the previous day.

While on his way to Darius' office, Andy wondered and worried about what they would be meeting about.

Andy tapped on the door and heard Darius walk to the entrance, where the shades had lowered.

"Andrew. Please come in. Good morning."

"Thank you, Darius. Is Katie still here?"

Before Darius could respond, Katie appeared through the doorway of the adjacent office.

"Yes. I am."

Andy was jolted by her red-faced, tear-stained appearance and sensed his news for them was not going to be as well-received as he might have thought.

"Katie...are you feeling poorly?"

"I'm trying to determine how I feel about all of the recent activities that will involve you and me."

"I understand your concern. I have had similar emotions."

"Please tell me of your thoughts."

"Katie, the greater picture of our future is full of wonderful opportunities. There is nothing but sunshine when I look into our future."

"But......"

"I expect that you are worried about my immediate challenges with the troops in Fort Dodge."

"Yes....I am. You promised that you wouldn't be taking off on all of these forays, putting yourself at risk and keeping us apart."

"Yes, I did...and I meant it."

"Then how do you justify coming to me to ask me for understanding...and approval?"

"With some minor exceptions pertaining to this upcoming trip, I will be traveling in the future as a businessman, not a lawman. I anticipate travel by train and coach...both of which should allow us to make some trips together."

"What about this upcoming journey?"

"You really shouldn't be along on this trip."

"I expected you would take that position."

"I expect this process to take about 30 days...not in its entirety but there are many aspects that would require my presence. Following that, I will have staff in place to take care of many of the duties. During that 30-day period I may be able to return to Wichita...indeed, I would think that returning frequently would be required."

"That explanation is almost exactly the same that my father presented to me over the course of the last 30 minutes. Did you two work together on this plan?"

"That would have been immensely more enjoyable than trying to come up with a plan and a plea by myself."

Darius chuckled as he nodded agreement with Andy's summary.

"Andrew, please commit to me that with your return and with your beginning a new career, you will also begin a new life that will allow us to be together on an almost daily basis. I just simply can't stand the thought that we would face a future that requires us to be apart so often.

"...and I so pledge."

Bob Harvey grew up on a small farm in eastern Colorado.....an arid region that prompted Bob to frequently quip that "you had to work hard just to raise a tumbleweed". The upside of that existence was that he was frequently picking up arrowheads, rusted guns, handcuffs and other historical artifacts that pointed to an earlier time when Native Americans, longhorn steers and drovers roamed the region.

He was a frequent reader of "Red Ryder" novels and comic books and later became a Zane Grey fan. His extensive travels in the states where the Chisholm Trail snaked through the hills and prairies offered opportunities to visit museums and communities where cattle drives were frequent....fostering an increased knowledge of the adventure and danger that was herding cattle.

ACKNOWLEDGMENTS

My thanks to Andy for continually bringing adventure and wonder to my life...and then to my wife, Judy, for helping to make sense of that adventure and wonder.

Special thanks to those who chose, and continue to choose, the life of the cowboy.

Last, but certainly not least, ol' Jesse Chisholm...patriot, pioneer and pathfinder... deserves some thanks for deciding to trust Black Beaver, a Lenape guide. The two of them took a take a path least travelled and they created history, its true, but they fostered a way of life .